BOMB POP THREAT

CRIME À LA MODE MYSTERIES, BOOK 3

CHRISTY BARRITT

CHAPTER ONE

"MOMMY, BOMB POPS ARE MY FAVORITE!" The six-year-old girl licked her Popsicle and grinned as she stood on the side of the gravel road with her parents. Behind her, a pale blue beach house rose from the sandy ground.

Serena's dog, Scoops, leaned forward and gave the girl a big lick on the face. All of that happened while the strands of "Sunshine Day" played through the overhead speakers of Elsa, Serena's ice cream truck.

Things couldn't have been more perfect if Serena was trying to film a commercial right now. The weather was gorgeous—not too hot and low humidity. The sky was a glorious blue. Even the birds seemed happy today. Instead of squawking like they had PMS, the seagulls circled in the sky and seemed to be singing along with Elsa instead.

Serena had a feeling it *was* going to be a good day. After a rough couple of weeks, she was excited about the Fourth of July celebration ahead of them. Festivities included an art festival and a mini-concert by pop singer Bree Jordan. The celebration would end with fireworks here on Lantern Beach.

The little girl's dad offered Serena a smile. "Moments like these make this island perfect."

"Like I always say, when all else fails, there's always ice cream," Serena said.

Seriously, she could be shooting a movie right now things were going so well. Where were the video cameras when she needed them? This day was gold.

Not only that, but she'd dressed up today like Annette Funicello from those old beach movies. She had her dark hair in two braids and wore high-waisted jean shorts and a red-and-white-checkered top that tied at her waist.

"I think this island is pretty perfect also," Serena said, one arm draped on her rolled-down window. "Where are you guys visiting from?"

"New Jersey," the dad said. "I know we have a

beach there, but it doesn't compare to Lantern Beach."

"Nothing does." As Serena grinned, she was certain everyone could see the sparkle on her teeth, almost like Hollywood magic had descended on her.

She pulled Scoops back in through the window and offered a wave before pulling away. She and her pup continued on her morning ice cream route. She hit the whole island first thing after breakfast, took a break at lunchtime, and then went back out in the evenings. It had been her routine for the past year, and it seemed to work for her.

Serena turned around at the end of the lane. Almost all of the streets here in Lantern Beach were dead ends. Then she headed back to the main highway where she would take a right and continue canvasing the area.

So far, this street had proven to be a red-hot sales area this week. There were lots of young families who liked to buy treats for their kids.

And for the parents. There was no shame in that.

"Get your ice cream before it's all sold!" she yelled out the window. "On a hot day, it's good and cold! Calories don't count when you're on vacation. That's my news to all the nation."

It wasn't her best pitch as she tried to hawk ice cream, but it was going to have to work today.

As she saw the steady stream of cars coming on the highway, she pressed on her brakes. She had to wait for an opening before she could turn—unless a driver felt sorry for her and let her through.

But before she could pull from the intersection, an explosion sounded behind her. Her entire truck rocked.

She looked into her rearview mirror in time to see a ball of flames spread into the air.

Her heart pounded against her chest.

What had happened?

So much for a perfect day.

She should have known it was too good to be true.

SERENA HELD Scoops in her arms as she stood outside her ice cream truck and watched the fire crew extinguish the flames. Several other families on the street were doing the same. Even people from neighboring roads had cut through yards to see what all the fuss was about.

From what Serena could tell, a birdhouse had

exploded. It hadn't been a cute little ornamental birdhouse but a practical one designed to attract martins, which ate mosquitoes. The insect could be problematic around the island, especially in the summer. Only the metal pole where the birdhouse had been perched remained in place.

When it came to things like explosions, Serena knew enough to realize that birdhouses did not blow up of their own accord.

Which left . . .

A bomb.

"What do you think, Scoops?" She rubbed her dog's head.

In response, the little canine licked her face. The dog was twelve pounds and some kind of terrier. He'd basically become Serena's best friend since she'd found him and then adopted him a few weeks ago.

Police Chief Cassidy Chambers circled ground zero around the birdhouse, pen and paper in hand. The woman was one of the best things to happen to this island. Serena had never told Cassidy this, but the police chief was her role model, everything that Serena wanted to be.

Cassidy had a position of respect and authority here on the island. She was strong, and she operated with integrity. Not only that, but she was pretty, with her blonde hair and slim figure, and she had married a Navy SEAL to boot.

The police chief glanced toward Serena, and her gaze narrowed as she started for the ice cream truck.

"I guess I shouldn't be surprised to see you here," Cassidy started, pausing in front of her.

Serena shrugged. "What can I say? I know how to be in the wrong place at the wrong time with the best of them."

"No one can argue that." Cassidy raised an eyebrow. They'd been through this song and dance way too many times before. "Did you see anything?"

"Other than the ball of fire?" Serena shook her head. She'd already thought this through. "I didn't. I haven't seen anybody at that house, as a matter of fact. But I'm pretty sure that Percy Smith lives there."

"Percy Smith?" Cassidy's eyes narrowed. "The man who owns the boat charter company?"

Serena nodded.

Cassidy lowered her pen and pad. "Now that you say that, I think you're correct. I assume he's not home at this time of day, but that he's out fishing."

Serena nodded again. "And he's not married and has no kids. Not that I'm stalking him or anything. I just happened to have heard Wilma Jane Lewis talking about how he's probably still single because he's such a miserable person."

"Interesting," Cassidy said with a stiff nod. "If you remember anything, let me know."

"Of course. It would be my honor."

Cassidy raised an eyebrow. "It wasn't an invitation to investigate, you know?"

"Oh, yeah. I totally know. I'm just a happy, beach-loving ice cream lady. Cowabunga!" Serena flashed her a hang ten sign with her hand, trying to portray her old beach movie persona.

Cassidy stared at her for a moment longer before nodding and stepping back to the scene.

But Serena's mind was already racing. What was going on in this town?

There was only one place she could think to go right now.

She wanted to speak to the new newspaper editor, Webster Newsome. He would want to know about this. The sooner, the better.

CHAPTER TWO

SERENA THREW on the brakes as she pulled up to Ernestine Sanders' house and saw Ernestine's nephew Webster Newsome step out with a suitcase in his hands.

She quickly put her truck in Park before darting toward him. Scoops remained on her heels. The neat freak's hair, which was normally combed away from his face, fell in his eyes. Sweat covered his brow. His shirt was partially untucked.

Weird. This was not the Webster Newsome she knew.

Serena stopped in front of him, panting just a little. "What's going on? Are you taking a trip?"

He shook his head as he heaved his suitcase into the trunk of his well-used sedan. "No. Not exactly."

Serena observed him. Saw the way his entire body remained tense. Listened to his clipped words. Watched his jerky actions.

Something was going on.

Her stomach tightened at the thought of it.

"Webster . . ." She waited, praying that he would offer some type of an explanation.

"I'm sorry, Serena." He slammed his trunk closed and turned toward her, an unreadable expression in his gaze. "I can't stay here anymore."

"You can't stay in Lantern Beach anymore? What do you mean? You've only been here a month."

He began walking toward his driver's side door, fishing through his pockets for his keys. "It's a long story. But it turns out you were right. I'm not the kind of guy who's going to fit in here on the island. I've decided to look for some job opportunities closer to the Raleigh area."

Serena sucked in a breath. She didn't know what to think. How could Webster be leaving? She was just figuring out how to put up with him.

She knew exactly what she needed to say to keep him here.

"But a bomb just went off at Percy Smith's house. We need to cover it for the newspaper."

He showed no reaction. "Talk to Ernestine about

it. Better yet, maybe you'll finally get that editor position you've been wanting." He paused and turned toward her, questions—and maybe a hint of sadness—in his gaze. "That's a good thing, right?"

Serena pushed a wayward hair behind her ear, her thoughts racing. "Webster . . ."

He let out a long breath before glancing away. "Look, I know this probably seems weird. I never should have come here. You were right when you warned me about that when I first arrived."

"I thought you were just starting to fit in more . . ." Her voice trailed. Why was she trying to get him to stay? Ever since he'd come, all she'd wanted was for him to leave.

Maybe Serena's problem was that she hadn't thought Webster actually would do that.

Especially not like this.

She picked up Scoops and held the dog close as she tried to process everything.

"So that's it?" Her voice caught. "Now you're going to be gone, almost like you were never here?"

Webster frowned, leaning against his car. "I am. You've got a lot of raw potential, Serena. I hope you keep writing because you're good at it. It was really nice to work with you for the amount of time I did."

"But Webster . . ." As she said the words, Scoops

barked in her arms, almost as if he agreed with her estimation of the situation. Neither of them wanted to let sleeping dogs lie.

Webster patted the dog's head, a far-off look in his gaze. "It was nice to get to know you also, Scoops."

Serena stared at Webster, trying to figure out what to say. But she was at a loss. Of all the things that she'd expected to happen today, this was not one of them.

Webster stared at her for just one more moment, something unspoken seeming to emanate from his eyes. But he said nothing. Instead, he opened his car door and climbed inside.

"I've gotta go," he muttered. "I don't want to miss the ferry. But I wish you the best, Serena."

Serena would be lying if she didn't admit that her throat burned right now. This was not how she had expected her perfect day to go. She had no choice but to step back and watch as Webster drove away.

She felt like he was taking a piece of her heart with him.

And that completed the transformation of this day from postcard perfect into totally bizarro.

SERENA STOOD THERE for several minutes, watching Webster's car disappear into the distance.

She couldn't believe this was really happening. Even worse, she hadn't realized just how much Webster had come to mean to her. She looked forward to their daily talks more than she wanted to admit.

It made no sense that he was leaving, and so abruptly at that. He wasn't an abrupt kind of guy. He was the type who scheduled when to floss his teeth every day. He put on his calendar when he needed to cut his toenails every week. Serena had caught a glimpse of his planner once, and the sight had been appalling.

She turned back toward Elsa. As she did, music began blaring from her truck.

"It's Raining, It's Pouring."

Serena gave the truck a dirty look.

How did Elsa always seem to read her mind? Not that Serena really believed that.

But still.

She started toward the vehicle but stopped herself. What about Webster's Aunt Ernestine? How was she dealing with this? And did she know anything more than Serena did?

Impulsively, Serena turned and stepped toward the little white cottage Webster had emerged from. She knocked on the door frame and waited. A moment later, Ernestine Sanders appeared wearing her signature linen pants and turquoise tunic.

But something about the woman's eyes looked different today. A certain brightness was missing, scrubbed away by . . . tears?

Serena had never seen Ernestine cry before. The woman could be colder than the frost-bitten freezers in Serena's ice cream truck.

"Serena." Ernestine pushed the door open. "I was wondering when you would come."

Serena pointed with her thumb behind her, not wasting any time with formalities. "Webster said he was leaving."

The lines on Ernestine's face grew deeper. "Come in."

Serena stepped inside and followed Ernestine to the screened-in porch, where the woman often worked. Ernestine didn't even fuss when Scoops wiggled out of Serena's arms and began to sniff around her house plants. Her normal rule was that Serena had to hold the dog if he came inside.

"What's going on?" Serena jumped in, desperate for some answers. Only a few moments ago, the bomb had dominated her thoughts. But no more.

Ernestine plucked a couple of dead leaves off one of her plants before sitting in a wicker chair and picking up her green smoothie. She frowned as she stared outside a moment. Even Elsa seemed to pick up on the woman's sour mood, and the music abruptly stopped.

"I'm not sure," Ernestine said. "Everything seemed fine this morning. Then right after I finished my coffee, I heard Webster slamming things around in his room. When I peeked inside, I saw he was packing his bags."

"Did he say why? That just doesn't make any sense."

Ernestine shook her head. "He gave me some kind of excuse about not fitting in here and said that maybe he could find a new job somewhere out near Raleigh. It was the first time he mentioned anything like that, though."

Something just wasn't fitting . . . kind of like trying to squeeze a new box of frozen treats into a freezer already stocked with the standard varieties.

"Did anything happen after breakfast?" Serena's

reporter instincts kicked in. People just didn't make decisions like this on a whim.

Well, maybe Serena did. But she knew she was the exception to the rule.

Webster wasn't an on-a-whim kind of guy. No, he liked his routines and schedules. He liked to do things by the book—so much so that it usually drove Serena crazy. What she wouldn't do to feel a little of that irritation now.

Ernestine shook her head. "No, not really. I had just overheard on the police scanner about the explosion on Laughing Gull Lane. I told him about it. Told him he should go out there so he could cover it for the paper. When I mentioned a pipe bomb, his face looked a little pale. About thirty minutes later, he started packing."

Why in the world would Webster have a reaction like that? It made no sense.

The realization left a sickly feeling in Serena's gut.

"I love my nephew," Ernestine said. "But, quite frankly, I was surprised he ever wanted to come here in the first place. He's always been very driven. And he made it clear that a small-town newspaper wasn't the life he saw for himself. He had loftier goals."

"Why *did* he come here to Lantern Beach?" The

words sounded frail as they left Serena's lips. She knew she shouldn't ask. She'd told herself she would wait until Webster decided to share that information with her.

But it didn't look like he would ever have that chance, so there was no need to hold back for the sake of future conversations.

"He didn't tell me." Ernestine frowned and leaned back in her wicker chair. "And I decided not to ask. Life is full of changes, and it's full of obstacles that sometimes force our hand at making those changes. I figured when Webster wanted to open up that he would."

"Of course." Serena couldn't deny the truth in Ernestine's words. Her own life was a reflection of that. Obstacles then change. Another obstacle and more change. That's when she had decided that she was going to start making changes on her own without life dictating her next move.

But so much still didn't make sense to her.

"It looks like I'm going to need you to cover that bomb that went off," Ernestine said. "Are you up for it?"

Serena hesitated, though she wasn't sure why. After all, this was the opening she'd been praying for, the road she wanted to take. So why did it feel like she'd taken a wrong turn?

She snapped out of her stupor and nodded. "Of course. I can start getting quotes from some of the witnesses. And I can talk to Cassidy and see if she'll give me an official statement on it. I'll do whatever I can."

Ernestine reached forward and patted her hand. "I know you will, my dear. I know you will."

Serena should feel excited. So why didn't she?

She knew why. It was because sometimes even people who loved change didn't love all change, only the change they could control.

CHAPTER THREE

SERENA DROVE a silent Elsa back to the scene of the explosion and talked to several people on the street, donning her reporter hat instead of her ice cream lady hat.

Several people recognized her and looked slightly confused at the switch. She couldn't blame them, and she was used to that reaction by now. She wore many hats. Literally. Today wasn't even one of her weirdest ones.

But no one she talked to had seen anything.

Just as she was ready to pull away from the street, she saw a truck pull up to the house where the explosion had occurred.

Percy Smith had returned home.

She watched as the man haphazardly threw his

truck into Park and then stormed up to the police officer stationed outside his house. The boat captain almost looked angry, with his heavy steps and red face.

Was that a normal reaction? Serena didn't think so. She would think that somebody might look concerned or bewildered or even in shock.

What was up with the anger?

The man was in his sixties, with curly salt-and-pepper hair and skin that had seen more than its fair share of sun. She'd heard from Wilma Jane Lewis that the man was a hothead.

In fact, the woman—who'd moved into town three months ago and apparently lived off the alimony her ex-husband provided—said that Percy had canceled her reservations for a private fishing charter. She'd been livid about it.

Serena had run into the woman at The Crazy Chefette and listened to her tirade.

Right now, Serena stepped closer, trying to over-hear what was being said.

She picked out a few key words, including pipe bomb.

"Why would someone do this?" Percy yelled.

"That's what we're trying to figure out, sir," Officer Leggott said.

"You better catch the person responsible." Percy leered at the officer. "What if someone had been hurt?"

"We don't believe that was the intention since the bomb was planted well away from the house and any vehicles." Officer Leggott raised his chin, despite Percy's in-your-face attitude. "There was no shrapnel inside either. Sometimes people put nails or broken glass in these bombs with the intention of hurting others. That didn't happen."

"Am I supposed to be grateful?" Percy shot back.

Leggott's face remained placid. "I know this is hard, but I assure you that we are looking into this."

"You better be," Percy growled. "Now, when can I start cleaning this mess up?"

Serena glanced at the "mess." Mostly, it was exploded pieces of the bird house. He'd also had a barrel of seashells in his front yard that had been turned over and a huge whale vertebra that had fallen.

All in all, it could have been so much worse.

Serena didn't know Percy well, and she'd never thought of him as being so unlikeable. Then again, she had heard that his fishing business was in trouble. Maybe to Percy this seemed like the straw that could break the proverbial camel's back.

Should she even try to get a quote from him?

Serena stared at the man as he stomped around, at his red cheeks and stiff muscles. She decided that now might not be the best time.

Was that what Webster would have told her? She thought the answer would be yes.

As she thought of Webster, her heart sagged again.

She should be happy. This meant that maybe she could become the newspaper editor. Ever since Serena learned he would take over as editor, she had wanted him to leave.

But now that he had . . . it just felt like something was missing in her life. She hadn't realized what a good friend he'd been to her since he moved to the island.

It seemed like so many of the people she knew here were married or had their own social circles. But when Webster came into town, the two of them had each other. She suddenly hadn't felt quite as lonely.

What was she going to do with herself now? Who would she hang out with and run her ideas past?

It was ridiculous really.

Then again, maybe Serena should have been careful what she wished for.

Now Webster was gone, and she already knew that life here on Lantern Beach would never be the same. Something about that realization made Serena want to cry, almost as if realizing a coveted cone of her favorite ice cream had melted and there was no more of that flavor in stock.

———————

SERENA AND SCOOPS went back to Elsa. As they did, Serena glanced at the time. She had a couple hours before she needed to start her afternoon ice cream route.

In the meantime, an idea nagged at her.

She pulled into a public lot near the Lantern Beach pier and put her truck into Park. As Scoops sat beside her, his head hanging out the window and watching the seagulls as they circled overhead, she grabbed her phone.

She pulled up the internet browser and began to type.

Then she stopped herself.

"I can't do this," she whispered.

Scoops wasn't listening. Instead, the dog fixated on a seagull who teased him, strutting only a few feet away in the parking lot and pecking at a piece of popcorn.

What had Serena been thinking? The fact that she was even asking herself these questions was ridiculous.

She should *not* do this internet search.

But if she was so certain she wouldn't find anything, then what would it hurt?

Still, Serena stared at that empty box where the cursor blinked, just begging for her to continue what she'd started.

Even if she typed the words, she wasn't going to find anything. She was being ridiculous. Over-thinking things.

She should just do the search and get it over with so she could move on. So she could prove that her theory had no merit.

Before she could second-guess herself, she typed in the words, "Richmond VA + pipe bombs."

Serena held her breath as she waited to see if any results would pop up.

She knew they wouldn't. She knew all of this was ridiculous.

As the results populated the screen, she sucked in a breath.

There had been a series of five different pipe bombs that went off in the Richmond area about two months ago.

Right before Webster had moved from the Virginia city to Lantern Beach.

Serena shook her head. She knew that Webster had been secretive. That he had been hiding parts of his past from her.

But she'd never imagined that he might be the one guilty of setting off bombs in the area. First in Richmond. And then he'd come down here.

Could he really be the one behind this?

And if he was, could Serena really bring herself to tell Cassidy?

"Oh, Scoops," she murmured. "What am I going to do?"

CHAPTER FOUR

SERENA DIDN'T KNOW what else to do, so she headed to Ernestine's place again. Maybe Serena would chat with the woman about her discovery. Maybe Ernestine could talk some sense into her.

As Serena climbed from her ice cream truck, she almost felt like she was dragging her feet as she started toward the house. She saw another car was here.

Clemson.

He was the town doctor *and* the Lantern Beach medical examiner. He and Ernestine had been seeing each other for a couple years now.

As Serena walked closer to the house, she saw the two of them sitting inside at the kitchen table. They looked like they were having a nice talk.

Maybe she shouldn't disturb them.

"What do you think, Scoops?" She looked down at her dog.

Scoops sat at attention and wagged his little tail. She wished her dog *did* have the answers she sought. Her canine was already priceless and had gotten her out of more than one scrape in the past.

Instead of walking toward the door, Serena paced the property for a moment, trying to work out her thoughts. Thankfully, Ernestine had a nice piece of property that would allow Serena to have some privacy.

On an island where land came at a steep price, Ernestine's lot had been handed down to her by the previous generation. She had two acres on Lantern Beach. None of the land backed up to the water, but it was still a great plot with numerous live oaks and good stretches of grass.

It was too bad that Ernestine never got outside to enjoy any of it. She was agoraphobic. Though the woman had made some strides in that area over the past couple years, she still had a long way to go.

Serena could envision kids out here running and playing football and chasing each other in a game of tag. Instead, it laid unused.

Behind the old cottage-style house sat an old workshop. Serena had never walked back there before, but she decided she'd stretch her legs just a bit more before she made any decisions.

As she got closer to the outbuilding, she saw that the door was cracked open.

Strange. She wondered if Ernestine knew about that. If there was anything valuable inside, the woman would definitely want this door to be closed.

Serena reached for the handle, about to pull it shut.

Before she could, something inside caught her eye.

She froze for a moment, unsure if she should follow her instincts or run away.

Her curiosity won, as it always did.

She pushed the door open farther and stepped inside.

On a bench in the workshop were . . . some wires. A timer. A steel water pipe.

And some . . . gunpowder.

The blood drained from Serena's face. It looked like Webster really might be behind the pipe bomb.

No wonder he fled town when he had.

SERENA TRIED to escape back to her truck before Ernestine saw her and asked what she was doing.

But just as she reached the ice cream truck, Ernestine stepped onto the porch and called to her. "Serena?"

She froze, wishing she could pretend she didn't hear.

But there was clearly no way to miss Ernestine right now.

Instead, Serena turned toward the woman.

"Hi, there!" She offered a large wave, trying to look more cheerful than she felt.

"What are you doing?" Ernestine asked, still standing in the doorway.

Clemson came and stood behind her.

"Oh, nothing . . ." Serena shrugged. "I was coming by to chat, but then I had an ice cream emergency."

An ice cream emergency? That was the best she could come up with?

Ernestine's eyes narrowed. "That's the first I've heard of those."

Serena shrugged. "What can I say? Some people get really testy when they don't have their favorite treat."

"What did you stop by to talk about?"

Serena froze again and considered her words. Then she knew exactly what she needed to say.

"I was wondering . . . Percy Smith has advertised in the *Lantern Beach Outlook* before, right?"

"That's right." Ernestine rubbed her hands together. "Why do you ask?"

"Did he and Webster ever have any encounters?"

"Funny you ask. They just got into an argument last week."

Serena's heart leapt into her throat. "About what?"

"Percy thought the advertising rates were too high. I haven't raised them in five years, though! The man is out of his mind."

"What did he say exactly?"

"That advertising rates like ours were eating up all his profit. He threatened to pull the ads for his business."

"I'm sorry to hear that," Serena said.

"Me too, but that's the way it works sometimes. What's going on?"

Serena stepped back toward her truck. "We'll talk more later. Right now, I have to take care of that ice cream emergency I told you about."

Before Ernestine could ask any more questions, Serena hopped into her truck.

Now more than ever, she realized she had to talk to Cassidy.

CHAPTER FIVE

CASSIDY STARED at Serena as the two of them sat at Cassidy's desk. "You're telling me that Webster Newsome is behind that bomb?"

Serena held Scoops closer, the dog feeling like a comfort blanket right now. "I'm not pointing the finger at anybody. I'm just telling you what I discovered."

Cassidy leaned back in her chair and nodded slowly, thoughtfully, before finally saying, "And there's bomb-making material at Ernestine's place?"

"That's right. I mean, I saw wires and a pipe and gunpowder. I don't know much about making bombs, but I do feel like I hear those items mentioned together on TV shows when it comes to these things."

"And you said that around the time Webster was in Richmond, there were also some pipe bombs there?"

Guilt pressed on Serena. Maybe she should have kept that to herself. But it was too late to take it back.

"That's correct. I just skimmed the articles. But the last thing I saw implied that no one had been arrested for it yet."

"And you said that Webster left this morning very suddenly?" Cassidy narrowed her gaze with thought.

"Also correct." Serena leaned forward. "Look, Webster is my friend. I know him. I can't see him doing something like this. But the evidence . . ."

Cassidy nodded. "I know it's hard when the evidence points to somebody we care about. Believe me, I've been in this situation before. So have you."

Yes, Serena had. A man on the island had died, and Serena's ice cream treats had been found around his dead body. She'd been certain she was going to spend the rest of her days in jail. Thankfully, she'd found the real bad guy first.

But would Webster also have that happy ending?

"What are you going to do?" Nausea squeezed at Serena as she waited for Cassidy's response.

"I'll get in touch with some of my colleagues up

in the surrounding areas. They can be on the lookout for Webster's car. We're definitely going to need to talk to him. And I'm going to head over to Ernestine's so I can check out these bomb-making materials myself."

"Okay." Serena shifted. "Is there any way . . . ?"

Cassidy raised her eyebrows as she waited for Serena to continue.

"Is there any way . . . my name could be left out of this?" Serena squirmed as the question left her lips. The suggestion alone made her feel slimy.

"You don't want Webster or Ernestine to know that you're the one who pointed the finger at Webster," Cassidy muttered, as if it were a foregone conclusion.

Serena nodded. "Maybe there's nothing to be ashamed of. But I feel like the most horrible person in the world right now. I'm not ready for people I care about to know that I turned him in."

Cassidy studied her face another moment before nodding. "I understand. I don't see why I would need to mention your name."

"Thank you." Serena stood. "It looks like I have some stops to make."

But before she could step from Cassidy's office, Paige Henderson, the police dispatcher, ran toward the door. "There's been another explosion. This time at Happy Hippie Produce."

"The Happy Hippie?" Serena's bottom lip dropped. That was her aunt's produce stand.

She had to get there.

Now.

SERENA PULLED up to the produce stand—a vintage Chevy van with a pergola extending from the side and little baskets out front. She threw Elsa into Park and rushed toward her aunt Skye, who stood out front with her arms pulled over her chest as she stared at her stand.

The good news was that it was still in one piece.

But something had obviously happened. Serena could still smell the smoke in the air and see a slight haze around them.

"Are you okay?" Serena rushed, looking at her aunt for any sign of injuries.

She saw none.

Skye nodded and ran a hand through her long, dark hair. Her husband, Austin, was already on the scene, and he slipped an arm around her waist. "I'm fine. The bomb wasn't near the stand. It was actually behind the dumpster and far enough away that nobody was hurt."

That seemed like a common theme. The bomb at Percy's place was also far enough away to make a statement but not harm anyone.

Still, the fact of the matter was that two bombs had gone off in Lantern Beach in one day.

But Webster was gone. How did these things work? Were the bombs set on timers? If so, they could have been planted in advance.

Serena bit back the emotions that warred inside her. She still could not see Webster doing something like this. But all the facts made him look guilty. Really guilty.

"What's going on in this town?" Skye stared at the remains of the dumpster. Firefighters were on scene and had put out the flames. Still, charred black ash had been left in the grass and on the dumpster.

"That's a great question. I'm just glad you weren't hurt." Skye was like the big sister she'd never had. Though they didn't hang out as much now that Skye had gotten married, Serena loved her aunt, with her Bohemian style and free-spirited attitude.

"It scared the life out of me." Skye shuddered. "One minute, I was ringing up some garden-fresh tomatoes. The next minute, I felt like I was in a war zone." Skye wrapped her arms over her chest and shook her head. "I heard about what happened at Percy's earlier. I just never thought that it would happen again or that it would happen here."

Austin rubbed Skye's back. "You know Cassidy will do everything she can to catch whoever is behind this."

Serena's stomach clenched tighter. Thanks to Serena, Cassidy's number one suspect right now was Webster.

How could things have fallen apart so quickly?

And if Webster wasn't behind it, then who was? And had this person set up Webster to take the fall?

Serena had so many questions, but not nearly enough answers.

But there was one more thing she needed to know—and it involved the link between Percy Smith and this produce stand. They were both businesses and/or business owners here in Lantern Beach that had been targeted.

Serena remembered Wilma Jane going off about Percy, telling Serena what a difficult man he was.

Whoever had set that pipe bomb must have really disliked Percy.

Just out of curiosity, Serena had a question for her aunt.

"Skye," Serena called. "Have you had any encounters with Wilma Jane?"

Skye shrugged. "She left a bad review of the produce stand not long ago. Why?"

"What kind of bad review?"

"Said the tomatoes were overripe. Said the service was terrible. Said Mother Nature herself would give this place zero stars."

Ouch.

"Why?" Skye studied Serena's face. "What does this have to do with anything?"

"I was just curious," Serena said. "I'll catch up with you later."

In the meantime, she added one more person to the list of people she needed to speak with.

Because Wilma Jane hated Percy and she'd hated this stand.

Did she hate both of them enough to set up pipe bombs to send a message?

CHAPTER SIX

AN HOUR LATER, Serena was back doing her ice cream route. As much as she wanted to focus all her energy on this investigation, she couldn't afford to do that. Her truck had been out of commission for a few days last week, and that had already set her back. She needed to try to sell all the ice cream she could.

She had already hit all her streets, as normal. As she did, she was on edge, waiting for another explosion to rip through the air.

Nothing had happened.

But the bombs were all that people wanted to talk about. Every time she stopped to sell more frozen treats, that subject came up.

Usually, Serena would be chatty. But right now, knowing that Webster might be guilty, all she could do was nod as she listened to people ask their questions.

There was a part of her that felt a little numb inside.

Webster couldn't have done this.

And Serena couldn't believe she'd told Cassidy that he might be responsible. What kind of friend was she? She understood the sting of betrayal all too well. Yet she was no better than the people who'd stabbed her in the back.

As she started down Percy's street, she pressed on her brakes when she saw the man outside, hosing down a small fishing boat.

He scowled when he saw Serena pull into his driveway, but he kept working, almost like he was trying to block her out.

When she remained in the driveway, he barked, "What do you want?"

Even Scoops seemed to notice, and he let out a low growl.

Despite that, Serena stuck her head out the window and leaned toward him. She reminded herself that she could catch more flies with honey—or ice cream—than she could vinegar. In other words, she needed to be sweet.

"Nice boat," she started, flashing a bright smile.

"Thanks," he muttered, still hosing the vessel down.

"I heard you were one of the best boatmen we have here on Lantern Beach." If she wasn't careful, this man was going to think she was hitting on him.

Tread carefully, she reminded herself.

"That's my aim," Percy said.

"Say, I was just curious . . . what do you know about Wilma Jane Lewis?"

His eyes narrowed even more, and he put his hose down. "More than I want to know. Why?"

"I heard she wasn't very fond of you or your business. Something about you cancelling a trip on her . . ."

"Is that what she told you?" Percy stomped over toward the truck. "What really happened was that Wilma Jane tried to make a reservation with me. But I know all about Wilma Jane. I know that all she does is complain."

"And that's a problem?" Serena asked.

"If I let her go on that charter trip with me, then she was just going to tear me up on social media. I've been trying to drum up business lately, and I didn't need her undoing all of my hard work."

"What do you mean?" Serena asked, trying to get all the information she could from the man.

"I mean, it's a well-known fact that Wilma Jane sees it as some type of power play to leave bad reviews. I didn't need her money that bad."

Serena nodded, letting what he said sink in. It matched what Skye had told her.

"You want to know something else I find interesting?" Percy asked.

"Do I ever," Serena muttered.

"One of my neighbors said that he saw Wilma Jane sneaking around my yard this morning right before that bomb went off."

Serena's heart seemed to miss a beat. "Is that right?"

"It is. I told the police chief. She is supposed to be investigating the woman. But as far as I'm concerned, Wilma Jane is responsible for this."

———

WHEN SERENA LEFT PERCY'S, it was almost like she was on autopilot.

She had a vague memory of where Wilma Jane lived. It was a newer house that was on the smaller side, with white siding and lots of interesting angles.

Kind of like Wilma Jane.

Under the guise of being on her ice cream route,

Serena decided to head toward the woman's place. What she hadn't figured out was a good reason to talk to Wilma Jane once she arrived.

Serena halfway hoped the woman might be outside when she pulled up. But that had been hoping for too much.

Instead, she put her truck in Park in Wilma Jane's driveway and strode up to her door.

Wilma Jane answered on the first knock. "Can I help you?"

The thirty-something woman had a round face and short bobbed hair that only accentuated the width of her cheeks. She liked to dress in bright colors that matched her loud voice but vastly contrasted with her sour disposition.

"It's your lucky day," Serena started. "You can have anything from my ice cream truck that you want."

The woman's eyes lit. "Can I? And why is that? I don't remember entering any contest."

"I put all the locals' names in a drawing every week," Serena said, making it up as she went. "You are the lucky person I drew this time."

"Oh, really?" She raised her thinly sketched eyebrows.

For a minute, Serena thought she would refuse.

But in the next instant, Wilma Jane trotted down the stairs toward the ice cream truck. "I think I will then. I do love a good Nutty Buddy on occasion."

As they reached the ground and Serena climbed into her truck, she questioned just how wise this was.

As a woman who liked to make business owners miserable with her nasty reviews, maybe working with her right now wasn't the best idea. Sometimes it seemed like the people who got things for free were the ones who complained the loudest about the businesses that provided those free things.

But Serena also knew she didn't have much time to waste.

"Did you hear about what happened over at Percy Smith's place?" Serena asked.

Wilma Jane prodded the top of the Nutty Buddy off and began to unpeel the paper around the edges. "I did. I heard it happened at the Happy Hippie also."

"It's terrible, isn't it?"

"It really is." Wilma Jane handed her trash back to Serena without question as to whether it was couth or not.

"What do you think happened?" Serena asked, placing the paper wrapper inside her truck.

Wilma Jane shrugged as she took her first bite into the Nutty Buddy. "No idea. Don't really care."

"I heard you two were friends," Serena continued. "In fact, someone said they saw you in Percy's yard this morning before the bombing."

She suddenly stopped mid-lick and pulled the Nutty Buddy away. "You heard that?"

"It's the rumor that's going around."

Her eyes narrowed. "It wasn't like that. I was going over there to egg his boat."

"Egg his boat? Why would you do that?"

"Because the man infuriates me. I can't believe he refused to book a charter for me on his boat. I had friends coming into town, and I heard he was the best."

"Did he say why?"

"He said he didn't like to work with difficult people." Her voice rose in obvious offense. "I thought that was discrimination. You can't discriminate against difficult people."

"And you were mad enough that you decided . . . to egg his boat?" It wasn't exactly a pipe bomb, was it?

"That's right. But my better sense got ahold of me. I figured I could do more damage through the written word than I could by casting stones . . . err, eggs."

"What did you do after you changed your mind?"

"I found somebody else I could take that charter boat trip with. We just got back a few minutes ago. My friends are upstairs getting cleaned up right now. Why are you asking?"

As Serena glanced back, she saw Cassidy pull up.

It looked like the police chief had just gotten word that Wilma Jane was back also.

But if the woman's alibi checked out, then she might not be guilty after all.

CHAPTER SEVEN

AFTER SERENA FINISHED HER ROUTE, she headed toward the boardwalk. Numerous vendors had come into town for Lantern Beach's Fourth of July celebration.

Historically, this week was always the busiest on the island. Who didn't love fireworks at the beach? Plus, the days were long and the weather was ideal.

Yet nothing felt ideal to Serena right now.

She and Scoops climbed from her ice cream truck and walked to the boardwalk. She just needed to clear her head a little bit.

As she strolled, she looked at the various vendors who were beginning to put up their signs. Serena had already reserved Elsa's spot, but there was no need for her to set up. On the Fourth, closer to the time for fireworks, she'd simply pull up and open her window. She had more than enough frozen treats ordered, and the optimistic part of her had visions of selling out.

Wouldn't that be nice? It would certainly help with some of her financial problems.

Tomorrow morning, she would also be interviewing that man who owned the company in charge of the fireworks. They had been coming to this island the past twenty years for the event.

Serena wished she cared. But right now she didn't.

Instead, she looked at the various tents and tables that were being arranged. There was homemade soap, seashell art, photographs, and air plants. That was just what she could see from where she stood.

Almost anything that you could think of would be sold here tomorrow.

Many of the vendors were from here on the island, but people had also come from other places to work this event.

Would these bombs scare people off? That was the last thing this island needed. But Serena knew that it was a possibility.

She snagged one of the bench swings that faced

BOMB POP THREAT 51

the ocean and sat there a moment, pulling Scoops into her lap.

How was she going to write this article? And would she mention Webster when she did?

No, she wouldn't.

When she'd been accused of a crime a couple weeks ago, at least her name hadn't been mentioned in the article. It had been a real lifesaver.

Though people deserved to know the truth, she couldn't ruin someone's life in the process. And that didn't matter if it was a stranger or a friend.

Until an arrest had been made, there would be no names mentioned.

Maybe it was time for her to get back to her place.

Plus, she needed to start writing this article.

Serena prayed that she would have the right words to do it justice.

SERENA LET out a groan and leaned back in the ladderback chair she had pulled up to her kitchen table/desk.

She'd already rewritten this article four times. It

didn't seem to matter what she said, the words didn't come out right.

Even if she didn't give Webster's name, his moniker still seemed to be written all over the article. Maybe she was the only one who would be able to see it, but the guilt wouldn't stop plaguing her.

"What am I supposed to do, Scoops?" She glanced down at her dog who lay curled at her feet.

He lifted his sleepy head and gave her a look that screamed compassionate. At least, it screamed compassionate for a dog.

Serena closed her laptop. Maybe she just needed a little break from all this. Her head was beginning to pound.

She glanced out the window of the little camper she called home. It wasn't even five hundred square feet inside, but it had enough personality for a place four times the size. There were teal cabinets, and stained-glass pictures in the windows, and fun tile work.

Her artsy Aunt Skye used to live here and had decorated it this way.

Serena loved it.

She frowned as she stared out the window. Darkness had already fallen. She'd probably been working on this article about the bombing for at least three hours now, and she should be finished. If it was any other article, she *would* be finished. But this one had her stumped.

Instead, she stood from her seat and stretched. Maybe she should just go to sleep. Maybe things would look brighter in the morning.

But without Webster here, she knew that probably wasn't the truth.

Who would she talk to and hang out with? Who would be the yin to her yang?

Nobody.

Serena knew that she would meet other people on the island. She even knew that she had other friends here. But no one would ever be able to replace Webster.

She hadn't even realized what a change of heart she'd had about the man until today.

Just then, Scoops let out a little growl and stood. His gaze was focused on her door.

"What is it, boy?" Serena felt herself tense. Her canine was a great little guard dog, and he'd obviously heard something that she hadn't.

Scoops' growl deepened, and he continued to stare at the door. The hair on his neck began to stand up. Serena's hair followed suit.

What was going on? Was someone here?

As soon as the questions filled her head, Serena heard a creak outside.

Someone *was* here. On her deck.

What if it was the person who'd left those bombs?

No, that didn't make sense. Why would that person come after her?

Serena's thoughts raced as she tried to figure out what she should do.

She reached into her drawer and pulled out a rolling pin. It would have to do. She didn't have any other weapons handy.

She crept toward the door, waiting to see what would happen next. Would her visitor try to get inside? Or was he leaving a present?

A bomb maybe?

Prickles dashed across her skin at the thought of it.

How did Serena keep getting herself into these messes? She had always been a curious girl. But she was only in her early twenties, and her life had already flashed before her eyes on more than one occasion.

She waited, her breaths entirely too shallow for comfort. As the door began to open, Scoops' growl turned into an all-out bark. The dog lunged from his seat and raced toward the door.

This was it, Serena realized.

Someone was trying to get into her camper.

She should have called the police when she had the chance.

CHAPTER EIGHT

"SERENA?" someone called.

Serena froze. She recognized that voice. Or was her mind playing tricks on her?

She wasn't sure.

She still held the rolling pin like a baseball bat, just in case. She didn't know what to expect here.

Because normal people didn't open the door to her camper without knocking then try to get inside.

Scoops' all-out barking turned into . . . a tail-wagging spectacle.

So much for her guard dog.

Serena squeezed the rolling pin harder, trying to anticipate what might happen next.

To her surprise, a familiar figure appeared in the doorway.

"Webster?" She lowered the rolling pin just slightly.

"It's me," he said with a whisper and a frown. "I'm sorry just to show up here."

"Have you ever heard of knocking?" she muttered. Despite the flippant words, she'd never been so glad to see him.

"I didn't want anyone to see me or hear me. Then I realized the door was cracked open, and I got worried."

"The door was cracked?" Now that he mentioned it, Serena may not have closed it all the way. The latch didn't always catch as it should.

Webster glanced at the rolling pin and raised his hands. "You don't think I'm here to . . . hurt you, do you?"

"I didn't know who was here." She lowered the rolling pin even more, trying to forget about everything she had learned about the man since he'd left earlier. "Why are you sneaking around?"

"Cassidy called me." He stared at Serena, his face laced with tension. "She asked me to come back."

"A lot has happened since you left," Serena said.

He pointed to the couch. "Do you mind?"

Serena contemplated the question for a minute.

But, in her gut, she knew she could trust Webster, despite what she'd learned about him.

Finally, she nodded. "Of course."

He shut the door behind him before sitting on the couch. He looked like he had been through the proverbial wringer. His face was pale. His normally neat hair was disheveled. Even his shirt looked wrinkled.

Serena had so many questions for him.

"Where did you park?" she rushed. "The police could be looking for your car."

"I left my car near the woods and walked over. I don't want to get you in trouble."

Serena lowered herself beside Webster. As she did, Scoops jumped into his lap and began licking his face.

It appeared that her dog had missed Webster too, even though he hadn't even been gone a day.

"Webster . . ." Serena rubbed her sweaty hands against her jeans, not even sure where to start.

He dragged his gaze to meet hers. "I know you have a lot of questions. I want to explain."

"That's good. Because I really want to hear your explanation."

WEBSTER TOOK a few minutes to gather himself before starting.

"First of all, I need to make it clear that I did not plant those pipe bombs." Webster turned toward Serena, his gaze still tortured and begging for understanding.

"You do realize that the materials for them were found at your aunt's house." Serena hoped she wasn't sharing too much information. But she also knew that Cassidy had already taken the evidence. Webster knowing about it made no difference at this point.

"Someone must have left those supplies there to make me look guilty."

This was beginning to feel a little too familiar. Someone had left evidence against Serena not too long ago also.

"Why would someone do that?" Serena asked.

Webster ran a hand through his hair and stared off, looking like he carried the burdens of the world on his shoulders. "Any chance I could get a cup of coffee?"

"Of course." Serena stood and walked to her little kitchenette, where she began to prepare Webster a cup. She knew that he liked to drink it black. She held off on asking any questions as it percolated. But plenty brewed in her mind.

She couldn't wait to hear what he had to say, and she really hoped his explanation was good. She wanted to believe him. She wanted to be on his side. But there was so much working against him right now.

Finally, the coffee finished brewing, and Serena handed the cup to Webster. He took a few sips, almost as if he needed the break so he could gather his energy before spilling the story to her. She carefully lowered herself beside him on the couch.

"There are things I haven't told you about my past," Webster started.

Scoops climbed up beside Serena and rested his front paws in her lap. "So I've gathered."

He pulled his gaze up to meet hers. "I really did intern at *The Washington Post*. And I really was an assistant editor in Richmond before I came here."

"What happened to make you come here?" Serena tucked her legs beneath her and grabbed a blanket, draping it over her. It wasn't even necessarily that she was cold. She just needed something warm and safe.

"When I was in Richmond, I came across a story

idea that I couldn't resist." He leaned forward, still holding the mug of coffee and looking into the liquid as if tea leaves might emerge and give him answers or clarity. "I was bound and determined to write the story. My colleagues told me I shouldn't. But I didn't care what they said. My heart was set on it."

"What was the story about?"

He let out a long breath. "There was a local airline-catering business that employed about two hundred people. Sky Gourmet."

"I've heard the name . . ." She couldn't remember why, however.

"One of the employees there came to me and told me about the working conditions at the factory. They were horrible. Low wages. Long hours. Unsafe conditions. Meanwhile, the airlines using them were raking in millions in profit. I knew there was a story there, that these employees needed a voice."

"So what was the problem?" Serena waited, anxious to hear the rest of the story.

"I'll get to that in a second. Let's just say, I found ten people who were willing to speak up about what it was like to work for Sky Gourmet."

"That was good news, right?"

"It would have been." Webster frowned. "Except my editor told me he wasn't going to run the article.

This company was affiliated with some of the newspaper's biggest advertisers. I knew my editor, Mr. Stoutkins, didn't want the paper to be on the outs with them, and that was exactly what would happen. The paper was already struggling."

Serena waited for Webster to continue, his tale already captivating her.

"I decided to run the story anyway. After Mr. Stoutkins left, I put the story in. I knew it was wrong. I knew I shouldn't do it. But these people's stories needed to be heard. There was no need for them to work in these conditions for such little pay."

Serena sucked in her breath, knowing that the story was going to take a turn for the worse.

"In my mind, the article was going to come out and I was going to be hailed a hero. Meanwhile, I just knew that the conditions at this company would change and these people would get the money owed to them. I wanted their lives to be better because I had taken these chances." Webster glanced out the window and frowned, looking for a moment like he'd been transported back in time to a very dark place. "But it wasn't like that."

Serena's throat tightened, and she rubbed Scoops' head. "What happened?"

"Instead of improving their work conditions, the

company fired the people who spoke against them." His neck looked strained, and his gaze even heavier as he glanced at Serena.

Serena's eyes widened. "Really? Wow. I'm sorry to hear that."

Webster nodded solemnly. "Me too. That was *never* what I intended for them. Out of the scenarios that played in my mind, it wasn't one of them."

"Nobody stepped up to defend you? To defend the workers?"

"No. Company management said the employees knew what they were getting into when they took the jobs there and that they should be grateful to have a paycheck. Meanwhile, Mr. Stoutkins was livid. Needless to say, I was fired too."

Serena tried to imagine it all playing out. Emotions twisted her heart at the injustice of it all. "That's horrible, but I'm not really sure what this has to do with what's going on here today."

"About a week after all that went down, pipe bombs began showing up in Richmond. At first, I had no idea that they were supposedly connected with me. But then I realized that the bombs were being left at the homes of people who were affiliated with Sky Gourmet. Somebody was taking revenge on the management."

She sucked in a breath. "Who?"

Webster shrugged, his eyes burdened with sadness. "That was the question. The police never caught the person responsible."

"But do you think it was somebody that you got fired?"

Webster shrugged. "It's my best guess. Eventually, a pipe bomb was left for me. That's when I knew I had to leave. I knew that I was putting other people at risk. All of that vengeance seemed to turn toward me."

A movie reel of the events began to play in her mind. It had to be horrible to realize those acts of violence had been because of him. He'd probably moved here to keep the people in Richmond safe.

"Did you tell the police all of that?" Serena asked.

"I tried to. But, believe it or not, it turned out the police chief was best friends with the president of Sky Gourmet. He didn't have very much compassion for me."

"That's too bad."

"That's why I always say we can't let relationships cloud our views. Justice is justice, despite personal connections."

"So you think the person responsible for this followed you here?" She tried to connect the dots.

"That's my assumption. Somehow, this person realized I was here, and he came to make my life miserable. He wants me to look guilty. He wants me to pay for what I caused to happen to him."

"If that's the case, then you should be able to recognize this person, right? After all, you interviewed everybody who was fired."

He nodded. "You would think. But there were a few other casualties. Probably forty people who were friends with the whistleblowers ended up being fired also."

"Whoever owns that company sounds like a horrible person."

"Jared Masterson. Oh, he is. I couldn't believe the greed I saw. I have to admit that I made some mistakes myself. I thought I could come here to Lantern Beach and start over. It looks like I was wrong." The frown that stretched across Webster's face made it clear he felt hopeless and like a failure.

Just as he said the words, there was a knock on the door.

"Serena!" someone called. "It's me. Police Chief Chambers. I need to come inside."

Serena glanced at Webster.

If she let Cassidy inside, then Webster would be a sitting duck.

But if she didn't . . . would she be aiding and abetting a fugitive?

What was she going to do?

CHAPTER NINE

"I CAN HOLD HER OFF," Serena whispered. She could stuff Webster into a closet. Cassidy would never have to know that he was here. He said he didn't park outside.

"No, you can't do that. You can't implicate your-self in this."

"But—"

"No buts about it." Webster stood, his expression grim. "I was going to go see her next anyway. I just wanted to explain things to you first. There's no need to delay the inevitable."

Before Serena could say anything else, Webster walked to the door. He pulled it open, his face that of a man who was about to receive a death sentence.

"Webster." Cassidy's hard gaze met his. "I thought you might be here."

"Hello, Chief Chambers. I was about to go down to the station. I just needed to talk to Serena first."

Cassidy pressed her lips together before saying, "Webster Newsome, you're under arrest under suspicion of making an unregistered destructive device and attempted bodily harm. You have the right to remain silent. You have the right to an attorney . . ."

Serena hardly heard the rest of what Cassidy said. She couldn't believe what was happening.

Was Cassidy really arresting Webster?

Scoops seemed just as upset about it as Serena did. The dog began barking at Cassidy and her accompanying officer as they led Webster outside.

"Webster . . . I'll figure out who's really behind this," Serena called.

"Do that," he said. "I'll be okay, Serena. Don't worry about me."

Serena wished it was that easy. But her heart squeezed with anxiety as he was led away.

When Webster was out of sight, Cassidy turned to Serena. "I don't think you want to get mixed up in this."

"I'm already mixed up in this," she told Cassidy.

"Besides, I thought you were going to arrest Wilma Jane."

"We questioned her," Cassidy explained. "But her alibi checked out. She's not our gal."

Serena let out a long breath, trying to think everything through. "How did you know Webster was here?"

"We found Webster's car in the woods. Then we followed his tracks here. It made sense."

"He told me he was going down to the station next." Serena frowned. "You've got to listen to his story. He can explain."

"I promise you I'll listen to his story, and I'll give him the benefit of the doubt. But right now, I need you to stay out of this. If Webster isn't guilty, that means there's somebody else out there who's leaving these bombs. If this person suspects that you might be affiliated with Webster then you might become a target too."

Cassidy's words echoed in Serena's mind. Her friend was right. Serena could be setting herself up with a bullseye right now.

But the only thing she cared about was helping her friend.

Webster had come back. And he had come to Serena.

That must mean that Webster had come to depend on Serena as much as Serena had come to depend on him.

She couldn't let him down.

———

VISITING hours were closed at the jail, so Serena knew there was no need to go there and try to talk to Webster again. Anything else would have to wait until morning.

Her heart sagged as she thought about Webster being in a jail cell. At least she knew all the officers in Lantern Beach and knew that he would be taken care of there. There were far worse places where he could be locked up.

But that didn't really make any of this better.

If somebody from Webster's past had come here to make him look guilty, then what was the connection with the people being targeted? That's what didn't make sense.

She decided to review what she knew so far.

The first person who'd been targeted was Percy Smith. He owned a charter boat business.

The second person was Skye.

There was really no connection between the two

of them except they both owned businesses here on the island—businesses that Wilma Jane wasn't happy with.

The woman seemed liked their best suspect.

However, Cassidy had ruled her out. After all, she'd moved here before Webster.

It only made sense that somebody from out of town was behind this. Most likely it was someone from the Richmond area who knew about what had happened. Maybe that person was on vacation here this week. The bomber must have seen Webster's name somehow, probably through reading the *Lantern Beach Outlook,* and had realized this was where he had moved.

But how would they have gotten the supplies to build the bombs? If this was something that had been spur of the moment when Webster's presence had been discovered, then this person wouldn't have had time to gather the supplies. And most people didn't come on vacation with various wires and explosives with them.

Maybe Serena could look into that tomorrow. Go to the hardware store and see if anyone had made any suspicious purchases while they had been there.

However, if that was the case, then this person

wasn't very smart. Certainly that was one of the first places Cassidy had checked.

Serena shook her head, feeling a headache forming. There had to be something that she could do.

And now that Webster had actually been charged in this crime, did that mean she *had* to use his name in the article?

She didn't want to do that. But that had been her litmus test. Serena had told herself that nobody would be named until the charges were official.

Since Webster had been arrested that seemed like a terrible idea also.

Serena let her head fall back against the couch. She had some big decisions to make. And she didn't know exactly what she was going to do. But she needed to figure it out, and she needed to figure it out soon.

CHAPTER TEN

THE NEXT MORNING, Serena wanted more than anything to jump right back into what was going on with Webster. But she had already lined up an interview with the man heading up the fireworks here on Lantern Beach.

His name was Chad Morrison, and the two of them were supposed to meet at The Crazy Chefette, one of Serena's favorite restaurants.

She hardly felt like herself as she'd rushed to get ready. She even missed her normal morning beach walk in the process. That meant she wasn't able to check out the daily seashell art someone had been leaving on the shores. If she had time, she'd go back later to see what today's image was. Right now, more pressing issues consumed her thoughts.

The fact that her costume for the day wasn't very original only confirmed that she was off her game right now.

She'd scrapped her original plan to dress like an American eagle. Instead, she'd opted to dress in red, white, and blue in honor of the Fourth of July. She completed the outfit with a headband featuring what looked like fireworks on top, along with a cityscape beneath them.

However, one of the "buildings" had serrated edges that almost looked like a weapon.

Still, it would have to work for today.

Maybe the fact that she felt off balance had something to do with the fact that she'd hardly been able to sleep all night. She'd been wrestling with her decision about what to do concerning Webster's arrest and the article she was writing.

When she woke up, she had no more clarity than she'd had when she tried to go to sleep.

But now she needed to put that out of her mind for a few minutes and focus on the task at hand.

With Scoops tucked in a little bag, she walked into The Crazy Chefette and looked around.

Only one man sat by himself, so Serena had to assume he was Chad. She smiled as she walked toward him. The man was probably in his fifties, with a thick mustache that was just beginning to show gray hairs through the brown. He had a nice smile and kind eyes.

"You must be Serena," he said.

She extended her hand. "I am. Nice to meet you."

"And who is this with you?" He nodded toward her bag.

"This is Scoops. As long as he stays out of trouble, people don't usually say anything about him."

"And that's the way it should be, right?"

"Absolutely." She slid into the booth across from him and ordered some coffee before she started the interview.

They went through the basic facts about how the fireworks show here had been a tradition for the past twenty years. As Chad told her about how the fireworks were set up, a conversation between two women behind her caught her ear.

"Do you really think Wilma Jane did it?" one woman whispered.

Serena tried to keep her attention on Chad, but her ear tuned to the conversation in the next booth over instead. She desperately wanted to hear their theories, to know if they'd heard something she hadn't.

"She can be very nasty," the other person said. "Maybe she was trying to make a point."

"Do you really think she has the smarts to make a pipe bomb?"

"Not at all. But can't you find everything online nowadays?"

"I still can't see her doing it for that reason alone. She's more the type to tear you up online or get into an argument on social media, you know?"

"Was she charged?"

"I haven't heard."

Serena had to agree with their assessment. Though Wilma Jane might have motive, she seemed more like the type to gossip than the type to react with physical violence.

She ignored the disappointment sinking inside her and turned her thoughts back to her interview with Chad.

All in all, he made an interesting story. It was just too bad that Serena had so many other things on her mind right now.

Nonetheless, she needed to get this written up so they could publish it this afternoon.

They'd already done some other stories on the Fourth of July celebration, trying to drum up publicity for the event. Hopefully this article would bring even more people over to see the show.

Serena knew that was what business owners really wanted and needed right now.

It was better than some of the other news articles that had run recently—some that had included a murder, the closing of a popular off-road vehicle ramp, and a ho-hum fishing season.

Just as she wrapped up the interview and stood, somebody rushed into the restaurant.

There was so much urgency in the action that it seemed like everybody who was inside turned to look at the college-aged boy.

Serena recognized him as one of the new life-guards who'd moved to the island for the summer.

"There was another bomb," he told anyone who was listening. "It just went off at the General Store."

Serena's stomach sank. How much worse could this get?

SERENA SAT in her ice cream truck for a moment, some little piece of evidence begging for her attention.

But what was it?

Percy Smith had been hit. Then the Happy Hippie. And now the General Store.

And Webster was in jail. He couldn't have left that last bomb.

Her mind continued to race. What did the three businesses have in common, other than the fact that they were all located in Lantern Beach?

That was when it hit her.

All three of those businesses advertised in the *Lantern Beach Outlook*.

Someone must have seen Webster's name in the newspaper and had begun to target their advertisers.

If the advertisers' businesses were hit and their profits therefore went down, then they would be less likely to advertise. Without advertisers, the newspaper couldn't stay afloat.

Someone was trying to ruin Webster just like Webster had supposedly ruined them.

That had to be it.

"That makes sense," she muttered to Scoops.

Scoops wagged his tail and let out a bark.

It was good to see that someone agreed with her.

But now that she had this information and a supposed motive, what could she do with it?

There was only one person she could think to talk to—one person besides Cassidy, at least.

She took off down the road toward Ernestine's. Maybe the longtime newspaperwoman would have some advice about what to do.

She pulled up to the cottage again and hopped out, Scoops right on her heels as always. She knocked rapidly at the door, anxious to talk with someone about this theory and to see where it might lead.

Finally, she heard footsteps coming toward her.

But not the light and graceful footsteps that she normally heard.

No, it didn't sound like Ernestine was coming to answer at all. The footsteps sounded heavier, more menacing.

Alarm rushed through Serena.

Who else was here?

And what if this bomber was now targeting Ernestine?

CHAPTER ELEVEN

SERENA TOOK a step back and reached for her phone. Maybe she should call the police.

But before she could, the door opened.

Webster stood there.

Before Serena realized what she was doing, she threw her arms around him. "You're out."

After a moment of hesitation, Webster's arms wrapped around her too, and he patted her back. "I am. The timing of the judge being in town worked out in my favor. My aunt posted bail for me, and I just got here."

"That's great." Serena stepped back and looked at him. He didn't look that much worse for the wear, all things considered. "So what does this mean?"

He shrugged, the action almost more of a twitch. "It means I can't leave this island until I'm cleared. I have a hearing coming up where I'll have to go before the county judge."

This was obviously still a long way from being over. "I'm glad you're out. I worried all night."

"Believe me, you weren't the only one." Ernestine stepped into the conversation. "Good to see you, Serena."

"I'm glad you're both here because I had a realization that I need to share with you," Serena said. "I'm hoping that you can help me figure out what we might need to do next."

Webster's eyes lit. "Of course. Whatever we can do to clear my name, that's what I need to do."

Ernestine's eyes locked with Serena's. "Besides that, don't you have an article to turn in?"

Serena's stomach tightened, but she nodded. "I've got my computer in the truck. I can send it to you in a few minutes."

"That's good. But I'm going to need the article on the fireworks also. We're cutting it close with this edition."

"I'll get right on that." Serena nodded, trying not to feel overwhelmed. "As soon as I finish talking to you two, I'll get that done. But right now, I need you both to listen."

AN HOUR LATER, Webster and Ernestine had agreed with Serena's assessment of the situation.

Someone was targeting their advertisers.

They had a list of at least eight other regular advertisers whose ads had run this week. Ernestine was not only going to call Cassidy, but she was going to call those advertisers and warn them to be careful.

In the meantime, Serena needed to get to her ice cream route. But she also had these articles to turn in.

And that was okay because she had the perfect solution.

As she and Webster walked from Ernestine's place, Serena tossed Webster her keys. "You're driving."

His eyes widened as he caught the keys, and his steps faltered a moment. "I've never driven an ice cream truck."

"No experience necessary. It's easy. I promise."

"But why do you need me to drive?" Webster

kept walking, but his steps were markedly slower now.

"It's twofold," Serena explained. "One is because while you drive, I can work on these articles. But the second is because there's no better way for you to see the people who are here in town than by patrolling in this ice cream truck. I'm like a cop on patrol, only a lot more fun."

"I can't deny that." Webster seemed to think about it for a moment before shrugging. "I suppose that's fine."

"Great. Let's go. I'm already late."

A moment later, they were in her truck. After some brief instructions, Webster headed down the road. As he did, Serena turned on the hot spot on her phone, logged into her computer, and sent the seashell art article, as well as the pipe bomb article, to Ernestine.

"You named me as a suspect, didn't you?" Webster's voice didn't hold any accusation. Instead, he almost sounded as if he simply wanted to know, to verify his assumption.

Serena frowned. "I just said that someone had been arrested."

He cut a glance at her. "You do have an obligation as a reporter."

"I know. And I fulfilled that obligation. I told people that there had been an arrest." Even as she said the word, a bad feeling gurgled in her gut. It was times like this she wished she didn't have to report the truth.

"But if this had been anybody else, you would have named names."

"But this isn't anybody else." Her throat burned as she said the words. "It's you. And I want you to have a fighting chance here."

"I appreciate that, Serena, but . . ." His voice trailed wistfully.

"There's no buts about it." She raised her chin, knowing her mind wouldn't be changed. "What's done is done."

Webster glanced over at her and his voice softened. "Thank you then. I do appreciate it."

"You would have done the same for me." Serena felt herself getting emotional and knew she needed to change the subject. She gripped her laptop as she glanced at him. "Now, I have really got to write this article about the fireworks. While I do, you need to be on the lookout for anyone who's familiar to you—or anyone who wants to buy ice cream."

"Of course. I can do that." His lips twisted in a frown. "But it seems too easy that I might actually recognize somebody. When has a suspect ever been handed to us that effortlessly?"

"We'll never know unless we try."

"I can't argue that."

"Well, let's get busy."

CHAPTER TWELVE

BY THE TIME Serena turned in her final article, Webster had already hit half the streets on Lantern Beach.

So far, he hadn't recognized anybody.

This wasn't going to work, Serena realized.

Sure, Webster was able to interact with a lot of people here in town. He was able to see a lot of visitors. But that didn't mean that the person behind these bombs was going to be out and about and buying ice cream.

Serena wasn't a math genius. But if she had to estimate the percentage of the vacationers here on the island versus the number of people who bought ice cream from her, she'd guess that maybe 10 percent of tourists patronized her business.

That left about 90 percent of the people vacationing here on the island a mystery.

They needed another plan. Serena knew exactly what that might be.

"I need you to skip these streets." Serena pointed to the road ahead, where several lanes full of houses ran perpendicular.

Webster glanced at her. "But I thought you needed to make as many sales as you could."

"I'm hoping that I will make up for some of these sales tonight at the fireworks. In the meantime, there's something more urgent I need to attend to."

"What could be more urgent than paying your bills?"

Did he really have to ask that? "Clearing you, of course. Now I need you to head down to City Hall."

"Are you sure . . . ?" He did a double take at her.

"I'm positive."

He still hesitated as he stole glances at Serena. "What's down at City Hall? And is it even open?"

"I heard they're working half days. I want to talk to the coordinator for the art festival."

"And why do you want to do that?"

Serena's hands flew into the air as she spelled it out for him, ticking off numbers with her fingers. "I know there are at least thirty vendors set up on the boardwalk for the art festival. Of those, probably ten are local, and another five are from various towns near us in the Outer Banks. What I'm wondering is if some of those other vendors might be from Richmond."

Webster's eyes narrowed. "Why do you think it's a vendor who might be the bomber?"

"I don't," Serena said. "But I've been trying to figure out a way to pinpoint who on this island might be visiting from Richmond."

"Okay . . ."

"My first thought was to go to the vacation management companies to see if they'd give that information up. I know they won't. Privacy and all."

"I'm listening."

"Then I thought, if we find a vendor who's from Richmond, maybe they've seen other people or talked to other people who are also from Richmond."

After a moment of thought, Webster slowly nodded. "You're probably right. I think it's worth a shot."

Satisfaction warmed her.

Serena *loved* being right.

Now she just had to hope that this lead didn't fizzle. She prayed it would lead to some answers.

LINDA LANGLEY STARED up at Serena and Webster from behind her overflowing desk. "You want to know where the vendors are from? I'm not sure I can give that information."

"It should be public," Serena said, adjusting her headband. "Most of these people participating in the art festival have the information either on their signs or on their business cards. It's really not a secret. It's not like you're giving out a home address. I just need a city."

Linda was in her thirties, wore oversized red glasses, and her hair always looked tousled, like she'd just woken up. Unfortunately, she came across just as ditzy as she looked. She always seemed confused and uncertain.

Right now, she stared at Serena and Webster, her eyes narrowed and her lips pursed. "I don't know . . ."

"Now that I think about it, aren't some of those cities listed on the brochure that you're giving out to people who are coming to town?" Serena snapped her fingers, suddenly feeling both proud of herself and eager.

Linda's eyes lit. "You know what? You're right. I think they are."

She looked through several papers in her files before she found one of those brochures. She turned to the back and looked at the list of sponsors before nodding. "It's here. And we do have two vendors who are from the Richmond area. One is selling homemade soaps, and the other is selling jewelry."

Bingo!

Linda jotted down the names on a piece of paper. "All of their booths should be opening at lunchtime, so if you want to catch anybody, that's probably the time."

Serena glanced at her watch and saw it was almost noon. "Perfect."

As they left the building, Webster glanced over at her. "Smart thinking. I just hope that it pays off."

"Me too."

"So what do you think we should do when we find these people?" Webster asked as they climbed into the ice cream truck.

"The first question you can ask yourself is if they look familiar."

"Neither of the names are familiar. But that doesn't mean that they're not a relative of somebody that I got fired."

"Good point. We'll have to be careful. But we can do this."

They headed to the retail area and parked. Serena and Webster made their way to the art festival.

Tables had been set up on the boardwalk. In the distance, she saw the pier. In the background, the Ferris wheel stood tall.

All in all, it looked like a picturesque scene. But darkness was hiding beneath all of this. Serena just needed to figure out where.

She scanned all the vendors until her gaze stopped on a table full of homemade jewelry.

That would be their first stop.

Serena started toward the booth, Webster by her side and Scoops on the leash in front of her.

She didn't always keep the dog on a leash, but in crowds like they were going to have today, she knew it was a must. She didn't want the dog to get hurt or lost.

But Scoops didn't seem to know what to do on a leash. He kept walking in circles like he wanted to have freedom but did not.

"Let me handle this," Serena whispered to Webster. "You just pretend like you're a doting boyfriend or something."

"Okay . . ." A wrinkle formed between Webster's eyes.

He really had to learn to do a better job at winging it. Not everything came with a twelve-step plan. Maybe she could show him the ropes later.

Serena walked up to the booth and began to look at the little feather-shaped leather earrings that the woman displayed.

If Serena had to guess, the vendor was probably in her early twenties. Serena didn't exactly see the woman as being someone who would make pipe bombs.

But Serena wasn't ready to rule anybody out yet.

"I love these earrings." Serena's words were the truth. They were super cute.

The woman smiled. "Thank you. I really enjoy making them."

"Are you set up in any stores? I don't have any cash on me, but I would like to check out your stuff later."

"I'm not right now. I just moved, so I'm still trying to establish myself." The woman pushed a blonde hair behind her ear, revealing she was wearing some of those same earrings Serena had been ogling.

They looked even cuter now that Serena saw them on someone.

But she had to stay focused. "Moved from where?"

"I was in Pittsburgh, but my husband just got transferred down to Richmond a couple weeks ago. I'm trying to establish myself there. I was so thankful I was able to get into this venue. I know it's not always easy."

Serena exchanged a glance with Webster.

If this woman had just moved to Richmond a couple weeks ago then she definitely wasn't the person they were looking for.

At least they could rule her out.

Serena grabbed one of the woman's business cards. "I'm going to look you up online then."

"I would appreciate that."

They continued to stroll down the boardwalk. To anyone watching, the two of them probably looked normal, like two vacationers out to enjoy the day.

How many people here knew what Webster had been accused of? Serena had almost expected to see more people staring at them. But no one seemed to give them a second glance.

Perhaps the news hadn't spread yet.

Just as that thought crossed her mind, Serena's phone rang. She glanced at the screen and saw it was Ernestine.

With a touch of hesitancy, she put the device to her ear. "Hi, Ernestine. What's going on?"

"I got your articles. The one on the fireworks is good to go. But the one on these pipe bombs is going to need some revising."

Serena glanced at Webster, who stood close enough that he could probably hear Ernestine's booming voice coming from the phone.

"Ernestine . . ." Serena's voice trailed.

"You know I want to protect my nephew more than anybody. But we have a job to do."

"But we're close to figuring out who's really behind this," Serena argued. "Really close."

"Are you really?" Ernestine's voice contained a good dose of skepticism.

Serena nibbled on her bottom lip a minute as she contemplated what she would say. "Yes, of course, we're close. We just need a little more time."

Ernestine didn't say anything for a moment until finally sighing. "Fine. I'm going to run an abbreviated article today. But tomorrow, I'm going to have to run an update and include the name of the person who was arrested. If you are going to find out who's really behind this, you need to do it today."

Serena ended the call and felt the pressure pushing inside her.

They had to solve this today.

How was that even possible?

CHAPTER THIRTEEN

SERENA FOUND the person she'd been looking for.

The Soap Shop owner, who hailed from Richmond.

The woman was probably in her sixties, and she had a wide variety of soap as well as some goat-milk lotion, all-natural toothpaste, and sugar-based body scrubs.

If Serena wasn't so intent on solving this case, she could probably drop some money at this art festival. It was a good thing she was preoccupied.

She picked up one of the bars of soap and inhaled the lavender scent. "This one's nice."

"It's so good for your skin," the woman, whose nametag read "Cindy," said. "It'll make it feel as soft as a baby. And there are no chemicals. It's all natural."

Serena wanted to buy the soap now even more than she had before.

"That's great." Serena looked down at the table at one of the business cards. "You're from Richmond? I have some friends up in that area."

"Yes, I love it up there. It's a great place to live. Although, I have to say that if I had to move, Lantern Beach would be my next choice." A smile flitted across Cindy's face as she stared at the shoreline in the distance.

"We love it here." Serena glanced back at Webster, who nodded.

His gaze didn't show any sign of recognition.

Serena turned back to Cindy, picking up a bar of orange-scented soap in the process. "How long have you lived there?"

"I moved there when I was eighteen, so for quite a while."

"Do you come to Lantern Beach often?" Serena continued, pretending to peruse the items on the table.

"I came here a couple times as a child, but it's probably been at least fifteen years since I've been back. I need to not wait so long next time. It's so lovely."

"I understand we have a lot of vacationers down here from the Richmond area." Serena was fishing for information, and she hoped this woman took the bait. Serena also hoped she sounded casual enough that she wouldn't freak the woman out.

"That's funny that you said that." Cindy leaned closer, as if she was about to share something important. "I've actually run into two people from Richmond just today."

Serena sucked in a deep breath. Maybe this was the information she was looking for. But she would need to proceed carefully.

"Really?" Serena muttered. "Isn't it a small world?"

"It sure is."

"My brother is actually thinking about moving to Richmond," Serena said. "He's been wanting to talk to a few people from the area to see what neighborhoods people his age are flocking to. Maybe he could talk to the people who are visiting from that area."

"Maybe. I'm not sure how you'd track them down, though. I didn't exactly get names and addresses." Cindy offered a hesitant smile, looking a little more cautious.

"Do you remember anything about those people?" Serena asked. "Maybe I could somehow track them down."

"I'm sorry. I wish I could help you out more. The only thing I remember one of the men saying was that he was staying over on Sandy Dune Lane. I only remember him because the street name sounds like a picture in itself, doesn't it?"

"It does," Webster said. "And you know what? I actually have a friend on that street. With any luck, maybe I'll run into this guy a little bit later."

Serena picked up the woman's card. "I may be back later to pick up some of the soap."

Cindy smiled. "I hope you will."

CHAPTER FOURTEEN

AS SERENA and Scoops hurried back to her truck, Webster skipped a few steps to keep up with her.

"Where are you going?" he rushed.

"The only logical place," she said. "I'm going to Sandy Dune Lane."

"And what are you going to do when you get there?"

She shrugged. "I'll figure it out as soon as we get there."

Webster didn't argue. Not that he had time to. Serena was now on a mission.

She felt so close to finding answers, and she couldn't back off now. Especially since Ernestine had imposed a deadline.

She climbed into the driver's seat of her ice cream truck, lifted Scoops into the empty space beside her, and reached for the keys from Webster.

"We should be careful here, Serena," Webster said. "We don't know who we're dealing with. And we don't want to go around throwing out accusations."

"I know that. I'll be careful."

Webster hesitated as he handed her the keys. She wasted no time cranking the engine and heading down the road.

As soon as she had hit Sandy Dune Lane, she decided to pretend like she was selling ice cream. It was the perfect cover for what they had to do.

"While I drive, you look for any license plates saying Virginia," she instructed.

"Yes, ma'am." Webster stared out the window at the different houses as they passed.

A man and woman flagged her down, and Serena pressed on the brakes. The two of them bought milkshakes from the new machine she'd had installed not long ago. As they walked away, looking like happy customers, Serena turned back to Webster.

"Anything?" she asked.

"Not yet. Let's keep going."

They continued down the lane. Finally, at one of the houses only one row back from the ocean, Serena spotted the Virginia plates she'd been looking for.

"That could be our guy," she announced, pressing on the brakes.

"Like I said, we can't jump to any conclusions here."

"I'm not jumping to conclusions. I'm just asking questions." Her eyes widened, and she pointed to the door to the house. "Oh look, someone's coming out now."

A man stepped onto the stairway beneath the house, a bag over his shoulder. He was probably in his forties, with a mostly bald head and a thick mustache. He didn't exactly look like the kind of guy who should be messed with. His muscles looked defined, and his tattoos definitely made a statement.

Serena pulled into the driveway, acting like she was turning around. As she did, she told Webster to duck before waving her hand out the window.

"Sorry," she called to the man there. "I just need to turn around since there's no other place to do it on the lane."

He nodded, acting like he didn't care as he continued down the driveway.

Serena pressed on the brakes and leaned out the window even farther. "Hey, isn't your name Frank Sealy?"

The man paused near his truck, barely glancing at her. "No, sorry."

"Are you sure?" Okay, it wasn't the most intelligent question she could have asked.

"Am I sure my name isn't Frank?" His voice cracked, like he wanted to say something biting but held back. "I'm quite certain."

"That's so strange." She kept her tone friendly and slightly ditzy. "Because you look like someone I know named Frank, who lives in Virginia. Small world, huh?"

"I assure you, I'm not Frank. I'm Aaron." He opened the door to his truck and tossed his bag in the back.

"Aaron? That's a nice name. Is it Aaron Sealy by chance?"

His gaze narrowed, and he didn't bother to hide his annoyance. "No, it's Aaron Stewart."

She stored away that information. "Okay, I guess it was worth a shot. I hope you have a great day."

His gaze was still narrowed as she pulled away.

As Serena headed back down the lane, she looked at Webster. "Did he look familiar?"

"No, I can't say he did."

"What about his name? Aaron Stewart."

"I can't say that sounds familiar either."

"Look him up on social media and see if he's mutual friends with anybody who worked at Sky Gourmet."

"You really can be bossy sometimes, can't you?" Webster stole a glance at her, a knot forming on his brow.

"Only when I feel passionate about something."

"I'm glad you feel passionate about this case."

Their roles seemed to have reversed. Serena had depended on Webster to help her with the last two investigations she had stumbled into. He'd also shown her the ropes of being an investigative reporter. Most of what she'd known she'd learned through on-the-job training when she first started.

It was weird now that he was asking her advice and turning to her for guidance.

But Serena kind of liked it.

"I found him." Webster straightened in his seat, as if excited.

"And?"

"I'm scanning his friends right now."

Webster didn't say anything for a moment, and Serena let him have his time. Instead, she decided maybe she could hit a few more streets while he was doing his research.

But they'd only gone two more streets when he sucked in a breath.

"What is it?"

"He's friends with somebody who worked at the factory. Someone named Addison Lane. She was one of the women who was fired."

Serena's heart rate quickened. "So maybe he's our guy?"

Webster glanced over at her. "He could be." He pointed at the screen. "Plus, it says Aaron used to be a bomb tech in the military."

Serena let those words wash over her. It looked like they may have found the guilty person.

Now the question was, what did they do about it?

FIVE MINUTES LATER, Serena pulled over on the side of the road so she and Webster could talk without any distractions. She, in general, could only focus on one thing at a time. Maybe that's why she and Scoops got along so well. They both noticed all the squirrels around them.

"What now?" Serena shifted toward him in her seat. As she did, Scoops jumped in her lap and waited for Webster's response.

Webster stared out the window a moment, his eyes flickering with thought. "I think we should follow him. If he is the guy behind this, then maybe we can catch him planting another bomb or buying some supplies."

"That's not a bad idea," Serena said. "But my vehicle isn't exactly the best one for doing these types of things."

"I agree. Let's go back to Ernestine's place and pick up my car instead."

"It sounds like a plan."

A few minutes later, they had made the switch. Webster was driving now and had even changed into a T-shirt so he would look more like a beach vacationer than a newspaper editor.

They parked on the side of the road, where it might look like they were just some tourists trying to get a good spot closer to the oceanfront. But, instead of climbing out of the car, they stayed where they were, waiting for Aaron to make his next move.

The more Serena thought about it, the more things clicked into place in her mind. All the times that Webster had looked so guarded. All the cautions he'd given her as far as how to approach newspaper stories. His determination to find the truth.

When she put those facts with what she now knew about his last newspaper experience, everything began to make sense. A more complete picture of Webster formed in her mind.

And knowing he wasn't perfect somehow made her like him more. Maybe it was because she was so imperfect herself. There was so much in her past that she wasn't proud of.

She'd never been a bad girl exactly. She had caved to peer pressure. She had cared what people thought of her way too many times. She had felt shame when she'd been rejected by her peers.

She didn't want to think that those things shaped her. But she knew that they did. All of her experiences helped to make her into who she was today.

"What are you thinking?" Webster asked, waving at a wayward fly that had sneaked inside the car and now flew at them like a drunken kamikaze.

"I just want to get to the bottom of this," Serena said.

It wasn't the whole truth, but her words were honest. She *did* want to get to the bottom of this. It had been quite the summer. She'd had many adventures since she'd come here to Lantern Beach.

So far, this summer had been her favorite. She just needed a happy ending to make sure that designation stuck.

"What if this guy doesn't leave?" Webster stared at the house in the distance with a frown.

Serena glanced at the time on her phone. "I have three hours until I need to be down at the boardwalk to set up for tonight's event. If nothing happens between now and then, I guess we will just move on."

She wasn't used to being the one who had to make these logical choices. That was usually Webster's role, and it was going to take some getting used to.

Webster turned toward her, and she could tell he wanted to say something. His gaze looked serious, his jaw hard, and his lips twitched.

"Look, Serena—" Webster started.

Before he could finish, she saw Aaron going to his truck.

"Look," Serena murmured. "There he is. We need to get ready to follow him."

Webster sat up straight. "We'll have to finish this conversation later."

Right now, they pulled out after Aaron Stewart.

Was he going to plant another bomb?

They were about to find out.

CHAPTER FIFTEEN

SEVERAL MINUTES LATER, Aaron pulled up to The Crazy Chefette.

Serena's heart caught in her throat. Was he planning on doing something to her friend's business? Lisa Garth owned the place, and she was seven and a half months pregnant. The thought of something happening to the woman made fire race through her veins.

Webster pulled into the lot and put his vehicle into Park. And then they waited.

Aaron grabbed something from his passenger seat and then glanced around.

"Suspicious," Serena muttered. Could it really be this easy? Were they catching this guy in his tracks?

Serena couldn't take her eyes off him. Instead of

walking toward the front door, Aaron strolled through the parking lot.

Was he looking for a place to leave the bomb? Was that even a bomb he had in his hands? It looked awfully small.

She reached for her phone, ready to call Cassidy. It looked like this was their guy.

But instead of heading toward another car, Aaron turned toward them.

Serena felt all her muscles tighten.

Aaron knew Serena and Webster were there. He probably knew they had followed him. And, based on his narrowed gaze and heavy footsteps, he didn't look happy.

Serena braced herself for whatever was about to happen.

CHAPTER SIXTEEN

"WHY ARE YOU FOLLOWING ME?" Aaron stormed over to Webster's sedan and paused outside beside Serena's window. The veins bulged at his neck, and his hands were gripped tight in fists.

Serena glanced at Webster, a sickly feeling in her stomach.

"I can take off now if you want me to," Webster muttered, his hand reaching to put the car in Drive. "Just give me the word."

Serena contemplated it for a moment before shaking her head. "No, that's okay. I want to hear what he has to say."

"The first sign he's going to get violent, I'm out of here."

Against Serena's better judgment, she reached for the handle and began opening the door.

"Serena—" Webster started.

"I've got this." She opened the door before he could stop her.

She was going to talk to this guy face-to-face, man to man. Err . . . make that woman to man, she should say.

But as soon as she stepped out and realized that the man towered over her by at least a foot, she second guessed her choice. She couldn't go back now. Instead, she raised her chin and locked gazes with him.

"We did follow you here," she started.

Her words almost seemed to surprise Aaron, and he took a step back. "Why?"

"Because I'm trying to figure out who's leaving these bombs all over town."

"And you think it might be me?" His voice rose in pitch.

"You used to be a bomb tech. Is that what you had in your hands when you got out of your truck?"

"Just now? No, it was my cell phone. I was looking for my charger." Realization rolled through his gaze. "You were trying to get my name out of me earlier, weren't you?"

Serena shrugged, careful to remain noncommittal.

His gaze darkened as he nodded, still studying Serena. "Normally, I might have words for you, but I have to give you credit. You're very clever."

She didn't take time to delight in his statement. Instead, she kept her gaze focused. "So back to the subject. You were a bomb tech."

"Bombs aren't something to be played with. I'm definitely not leaving them all over town."

"But you were also friends with Addison Lane."

He scratched the back of his head and shrugged. "What does Addison have to do with this? We went to high school together."

"When was the last time you talked to her?" Serena pushed.

"It's probably been eight years if I had to guess."

Years? That didn't bode well for her theory.

"I see." Serena crossed her arms, trying to think of another argument or another reason why this man might be guilty.

"What's this about?" He crept closer, some of his friendliness disappearing. "I've cooperated with you. Now it's your turn."

"She used to work for Sky Gourmet," Serena said. "We believe someone who worked for that company or who is associated with someone who worked for that company is now setting off pipe bombs here in Lantern Beach."

"And since Addison worked for them, and I know Addison—"

"And you were a bomb tech," Serena added.

"You thought I was involved." He crossed his arms and shook his head, a disapproving look in his gaze. "You were wrong."

"You can see where we might have drawn a conclusion like this," Serena insisted.

"Maybe. But I didn't get into town until yesterday at lunchtime. Didn't the first bomb go off before that?"

Doggonit! He was right. If his story checked out, then he couldn't be their guy.

That left Webster and Serena right back at square one.

Disappointment bit deep. Serena had really thought they were onto something.

Apparently, she still had more work to do before she could call herself an ace investigator.

CHAPTER SEVENTEEN

SERENA AND WEBSTER headed back to Ernestine's to talk through things before Serena had to be back to sell ice cream at the fireworks celebration. Webster had called his aunt and given her a brief update earlier. They would fill in all the new details now.

Webster and Serena had little to say on the short drive to his aunt's house. What was there to talk about?

Serena had been wrong.

Of course, the two of them still needed to verify this Aaron guy's alibi. But if he was telling the truth, then they'd just wasted valuable time.

Before going into Ernestine's house, Serena climbed into her ice cream truck and pulled out a few treats for them. She got a fruit bar for Ernestine, who tried to eat healthy; an ice cream sandwich for Webster, knowing it was his favorite; a Creamsicle for Scoops; and Serena got a . . . Bomb Pop.

Maybe it wasn't the best choice for times like this, but it sounded really good on a hot day like today. Besides, ice cream always made everything better.

They all sat in Ernestine's sunroom, munching on their treats as they spoke.

"Did you contact all the businesses who have advertised in our newspaper?" Serena started.

"I did," Ernestine said. "I warned them all. And they thanked us for giving them the heads up."

"What about Cassidy?" Webster asked. "Did you fill her in also?"

"I did. She said she'd have an officer patrol those businesses to make sure nothing happened. She's also going to send out some officers to look around the properties and to make sure that something hasn't already been planted."

"Glad to hear that."

"Where does this leave us?" Serena asked. "Who else do we need to be looking at?"

Ernestine cleared her throat. "I did find out one thing that I thought you might want to know."

"What's that?" Webster leaned toward her, crumbling his ice cream sandwich wrapper and shooting it into a nearby trashcan.

"I looked into that woman who makes and sells those soaps," Ernestine said. "I figured it was worth a shot."

"What did you find out about her?" Serena asked.

Ernestine's eyes lit, like she had discovered something good. "It turns out she has a criminal record."

Serena sat up straighter. She hadn't expected to hear that news. "A criminal record for what?"

"Apparently, she was involved with a pretty violent protest about twenty years ago."

"Protest over what?" Webster asked.

"Had something to do with animal rights. But you know there's been a lot of fuss on the island right now over our piping plovers. Those birds have closed down some of our off-road vehicle ramps, and some people aren't happy about it."

"But then what does that have to do with Webster or the newspaper?" Serena asked.

"We covered the story. In fact, we ran an editorial in support of the fishermen who think that those off-road vehicle ramps should be open. Maybe she's upset about it."

"Then why plant evidence on your property?" Serena asked.

Ernestine's gaze met Serena's. "Did you ever think that maybe it wasn't Webster who was meant to be implicated, but me? Or, for that matter, maybe she did know what happened to Webster in Richmond. Maybe she thought he would be a good scapegoat for all of this."

Serena leaned back as she processed Ernestine's words. "Well, it's one theory."

"I'm not saying that I'm right," Ernestine continued. "I'm just saying we need to investigate all the angles that we possibly can."

"I agree," Serena said.

Webster glanced at Serena and then at his aunt. "So what now?"

Serena glanced at the time. "Bree Jordan's concert should be wrapping up. That means I need to get to the fireworks. I might see if my aunt can help me out while I'm there. I would like to keep my eyes and ears open as to what's going to happen. I don't think this person is finished yet."

"I think you're right," Ernestine said. "I wish I could get out there and help you."

As she frowned, Serena saw the internal struggle. Dealing with agoraphobia couldn't be easy. Last

Serena had heard, Ernestine and Clemson planned on staying at her house to watch the fireworks from here.

"We'll do our best," Serena said. "Don't worry about us."

Ernestine nodded. "You've got to find out who's doing this. I can't have my nephew go to jail for a crime he didn't commit."

SKYE AGREED to help Serena out at her ice cream truck. While her aunt and Austin manned that for an hour or two, Serena and Webster wandered down the boardwalk toward Cindy's soap table.

They stopped several feet away, close enough to keep an eye on Cindy. The crowds were bustling on the boardwalk. On the other side of the walkway, people were leaving the Bree Jordan concert.

There were certainly a lot of people out and about. Maybe that would make it easier for Webster and Serena to remain concealed as they stood near one of the swings facing the ocean.

Serena watched Cindy now. She just seemed so sweet. Serena couldn't imagine the woman being arrested for a protest, nor could she imagine the woman building bombs. But sometimes it was the person who seemed the least likely to do things like that who was guilty. Serena had learned that in the past.

As she glanced down the boardwalk, she spotted several officers patrolling the area. It was getting dark outside right now, but they still had at least an hour until the fireworks would go off. An entire section of the beach had been roped off, and nobody was allowed to go in that area because the fireworks had been set up there.

Serena just prayed that nothing would go wrong tonight. There had already been enough destruction. Thankfully, nobody had been hurt yet. But would they be that lucky next time?

It seemed like they were already pushing the limits.

"I have a bad feeling in my gut." Webster crossed his arms as he stared at Cindy's booth.

"Me too." Serena held on to Scoops' leash.

"I guess we just wait and see what's going to happen." Serena pushed her sunglasses up higher, hoping they would make it less obvious that she was watching the people around her. "Or we get close enough that maybe we can hear anything that the cops say. We can also keep an eye on Cindy."

"Right now, I guess Cindy is our best suspect," Webster said.

"We haven't had time to prove Aaron's alibi yet. But I'm not ruling him out."

"And if the two of them didn't do this?" Webster glanced at Serena.

That was an excellent question . . . "Then it could be somebody that we haven't even discovered yet. It's really hard to say in these kinds of situations. What about your editor? Or the owner of Sky Gourmet? They seem like men who would have obvious vendettas against you."

"True, but I have no way of knowing if either of them is here right now."

His words were true. It was difficult to scope out exactly who was on the island. Yet, at the same time, they couldn't leave it to chance that they'd run into the bomber.

Webster let out a long breath, and Serena could tell that he was anxious.

She didn't blame him. She would be the same way if she was in his shoes.

As they waited, the tension inside her continued to grow.

So far, there had been nothing. No signs of who

might be guilty. Not a single thing that seemed suspicious.

Serena didn't know whether to delight in that news or to find frustration in it. Though she didn't want any more bombs to go off, unless something else happened, she feared they might not ever find the bad guy.

Just as the thought entered her mind, she heard the radio crackle on one of the police officers' belts. Nearby, the officer raised the radio to his ear.

Serena stepped closer, pretending like Scoops pulled her that way.

"Another bomb went off?" the officer said.

Webster and Serena glanced at each other.

The officer on the other end of the radio rattled off an address. "I'll be right there."

Serena knew what she had to do.

She stepped closer to Webster so no one else could overhear. "You stay here and keep an eye on Cindy. I'm going to take your car and see what's going on at this new bomb site."

"Are you sure?" Webster blinked, his expression showing his uncertainty.

"I'm positive. Don't do anything that I wouldn't do."

"And that would limit me how?" A hint of amusement laced his voice.

Serena punched his shoulder. "Very funny. Now, Scoops and I have to go. We don't have any time to waste."

.

CHAPTER EIGHTEEN

SERENA FOLLOWED behind the police car, even though she didn't have to. She had heard the address, and she knew exactly where she was going.

Who had the bomber targeted this time? Ernestine had given warning to all their regular advertisers. But was there someone that they had missed?

Serena kept turning the address over in her mind, wondering why it seemed kind of familiar.

A few minutes later, she saw a fire truck and two police cars parked in front of a residence.

Not just any residence.

It was the only inn located in Lantern Beach.

The innkeeper paced out front as firefighters cleared any gawkers from the scene.

Serena glanced around. Where had the bomb gone off?

Finally, she saw an area near where an ornamental well had sat on the side of the building. Except the well was no longer there.

Somebody had set the bomb up there, she realized.

Was the inn one of the newspaper's advertisers? Serena didn't think so.

So why had this place been targeted? It didn't make sense.

She remained in the distance as Cassidy came onto the scene to investigate.

As she did, Serena glanced around. Was the person responsible for this attack here right now? Was he standing in the background, watching his handiwork?

Serena couldn't be sure. As she glanced around, she didn't see anyone out of the ordinary. It was mostly tourists and gawkers who were wondering what was going on.

But one person across the way caught her eye.

Aaron Stewart stood there. What was he doing near the inn?

Maybe she should have taken the time to check out his alibi sooner.

When he saw her, he took off into a run.

Serena knew she was too far away to catch him now.

But she planned on tracking him down as soon as she could.

SERENA AND SCOOPS got back to the boardwalk and stopped at the area where she had left Webster.

He was gone.

She glanced around. He must have just wandered away for a moment.

But Serena didn't see him anywhere.

Out of curiosity, she dialed Webster's cell phone number.

He didn't answer.

Weird.

She wandered over to Elsa and squeezed in between the long line there.

"Have you seen Webster?" she asked Skye.

Her aunt frowned as she handed someone a banana split. "No. Sorry. But we've been slammed. You owe us."

"Yes, I do." She'd have to pay her debt with Skye

and Austin later. "Look, if you see Webster, can you tell him I'm looking for him?"

"Of course."

Turning back to the crowd, a bad feeling formed in Serena's gut.

Her phone rang. Her breath caught—until she looked at the caller ID.

It was Ernestine.

"Anything new?" the woman asked.

"You heard about what happened at the inn?" Serena asked.

"I did."

"But they didn't advertise with us." Serena still couldn't figure that one out.

"No, but they're sponsoring the special Fourth of July issue that just came out," Ernestine said. "Somehow, their name got left off the list."

That only seemed to confirm that someone was targeting newspaper advertisers—for the purpose of making Webster suffer.

This wasn't good.

Serena promised Ernestine she'd call with any updates, and then she glanced at the time again. Fireworks were supposed to start in ten minutes.

What happened during the time Serena was

gone? And why wasn't Webster answering his phone?

She began pacing the boardwalk with Scoops, searching all the faces there for Webster.

But she didn't see him anywhere.

She paused near Cindy's soap booth. The woman also had a long line there. Serena seriously doubted that the woman had been able to leave or distract Webster. Cindy appeared to be a one-woman show.

In Serena's gut, she didn't think she was responsible for any of this.

But then from across the way she spotted Aaron Stewart. When he'd left the inn, he'd come back here.

And Serena wanted to know why.

Before he could get away from her, she ran through the crowd. "Hey!"

He turned back at her, and his eyes widened.

Serena was afraid that he might run.

CHAPTER NINETEEN

"WHAT DO YOU WANT NOW?" Aaron growled.

Serena caught her breath as she stopped in front of him. At least he hadn't run. "Have you seen my friend?"

"What friend?" His voice rose.

He obviously thought she was an idiot.

"The one I was with earlier." Serena drew in another ragged breath.

"No. Why would I have seen him?"

She narrowed her gaze, wondering why he was the one playing stupid right now. "You were at the inn when the explosion went off. What were you doing there?"

His gaze narrowed. "I wasn't leaving a bomb, if that's what you think."

"Then what were you doing?"

He let out a long breath. "If you must know, I overheard that there had been another explosion. I am a certified bomb tech. And I told the chief of police that. I went to see if there was anything I could do to help."

Part of her wanted to believe him but . . . "Why did you run when you saw me?"

"Run? I didn't run. I saw you, and I continued walking, like I had started to do before you saw me. I did nothing wrong, and I'm certainly not a vigilante trying to ruin people's lives."

Serena studied him. He seemed to be telling the truth.

But if that was the case, she really wasn't getting anywhere with this investigation, was she?

And she still hadn't found Webster.

Where had the man gone?

Worry grew inside her.

She glanced back at Aaron, knowing that he hadn't had time to do anything to Webster while she was gone. She could clear him in that regard, at least.

"Thanks for your help," she muttered.

But right now, she just needed to find her friend.

As Serena turned to leave, she almost collided

with Linda, the coordinator of the Fourth of July celebration. The woman held a clipboard in her hands and wore a headset over her ears. She looked distracted as she wandered down the boardwalk.

"Oh, Serena. I didn't mean to nearly hit you." She let out a feeble laugh.

"It's okay." Serena had much bigger worries on her mind right now.

"I'm glad I ran into you," Linda said, glancing at her clipboard again. "Because there's one more person I thought of who has a connection to Richmond."

"Who's that?" Serena's heart raced as she waited for her answer.

When Serena heard who it was, she couldn't believe her ears.

How had she not connected this earlier?

———

"SCOOPS, we have got to find Webster. Now."

Scoops barked in response and began tugging on the leash.

Serena hadn't actually thought that he would understand her, but Scoops seemed to know exactly where he was going.

As the canine led her through the crowds, Serena pulled out her phone. If her theory was right, she couldn't face this on her own.

She was going to need backup.

A lot of it.

She dialed Cassidy's number, but the police chief didn't answer. No doubt she was still at the crime scene, probably talking to people and gathering evidence at the inn.

Next, Serena tried the police station.

Paige, the dispatcher, answered, "Lantern Beach PD. What's your emergency?"

"Paige, this is Serena Lavinia. I really need to talk to Cassidy."

"She's not here right now, but I can pass on a message to her."

"It's urgent. It's about this bomber. I'm down at the firework site, and I think I know who it is. Please, have her call me right away. Better yet—have her come here."

"Okay, I'll see if I can contact her right now."

Serena slid her phone back into her pocket as Scoops continued to pull her.

Finally, the crowds ended.

But a police line had been set up, blocking this area from any pedestrians.

How was Serena going to get past the officers stationed there? Should she enlist their help? She was just going on a hunch here, and these guys had no reason to trust her.

Besides, Cassidy should be here soon . . . hopefully.

"Oh, look at the cute little dog." One of the officers bent down to pet Scoops.

These weren't the normal Lantern Beach officers, but backup from the state police had been called in.

As the officer rubbed Scoops' head, the leash slipped from Serena's hands.

Slipped being the operative word here.

Scoops scooted under the police line and began running down the dark beach on the other side.

"Hey!" the officer called.

While the man was distracted, Serena slipped under the police line too and took off after her dog.

"Scoops!" she called.

"You can't be over there!" the officer called.

"I've got to get my dog," she yelled back.

Serena didn't slow her steps. She couldn't afford to.

She had to keep moving.

She thought she heard footsteps behind her,

pounding through the sand. But she kept moving. Kept chasing after Scoops.

And hopefully getting closer to Webster.

"Good boy," she muttered to herself.

When she had found Scoops, she had found the best crime-fighting partner in the world.

Scoops ran off the beach in between some houses. As Serena chased after him, the cops behind her seemed to fade away.

She hoped, at least.

But where was Scoops going?

Her legs burned as she tried to keep up with the canine. Just when she had no idea what the dog was doing, he circled around the house and went back to the beach.

As they reached the new area, she stopped in her tracks.

Racks of fireworks had been set up in the sand. It was nearly impossible to see them because it was so dark. But, every once in a while, someone wandered past with a flashlight, and that's when Serena saw the details.

She tried to remember what Chad Morrison, the owner of the pyrotechnic company, had told her.

Each rack, which almost looked like a wooden pallet-like box, contained two rows of fireworks, five canisters in each row. The canisters varied in size, depending on how big the firework shell was.

For this show, there was going to be four hundred fifty fireworks that would go off over a period of twelve minutes.

Each one of the fireworks was basically an explosive. A fuse was set on each of the racks that would allow the fireworks to go off.

While some pyro teams had automated sequences, Chad's team lit each firework sequence manually using a road flare or a small blow torch.

She walked toward the edge of the firework display and pulled up the flashlight on her phone.

She shined it up and down the various racks.

She sucked in a breath at what she saw at one of the racks toward the end.

Webster.

He'd been tied to one of the wooden racks full of explosive fireworks.

The show was slated to start at any minute.

At any minute, the fireworks would explode and Webster would die.

CHAPTER TWENTY

SERENA RUSHED TOWARD WEBSTER.

His eyes lit when he spotted her. Quickly, she pulled the gag from his mouth.

"Serena . . . you have to be careful," Webster said, tugging against the binds holding him in place. "He'll be back anytime now."

She tugged at the rope, trying to get the knot out. A useless effort. It was too tight.

As the first explosion filled the air, her heart raced.

They were going to run out of time soon. This whole show lasted only twelve minutes. It wasn't safe to be here.

She glanced at the other end of the display and saw the glow of red lights as the pyro team lit various tracks. She could call for help, but she didn't know if she could trust them. Besides, they all wore ear plugs to protect their hearing. It was so dark out here, these guys probably didn't even see anything over on this end.

Webster was positioned out of sight.

Could one of these guys light the fuse on the other end of the rack without ever knowing he was there? She didn't know, but she couldn't take that chance.

Wasn't that exactly what Chad Morrison wanted? For this to look like a tragic accident?

Serena's stomach sank at the thought.

She couldn't believe she hadn't seen it earlier.

"What happened?" she asked Webster as she worked the knot.

"Can we talk about that later? Maybe we should call the police now."

"I did. With any luck, Cassidy will be here at any time."

"With any luck?" Webster's voice cracked. "No offense, but that doesn't fill me with confidence."

"I'm offended," Serena said before smiling and letting him know she was kidding. "Sorry, but I'm doing the best I can."

"I know you are. Thanks for coming."

Serena glanced at Scoops, who let out a little whine with every explosion. Her heart sank.

The explosions continued to go off. If something happened . . . she couldn't keep her dog here.

She let go of the leash. "Go, boy!"

The dog stared at her.

"Go, Scoops." She continued to work the knot.

As she did, the explosions rattled her chest. Her eardrums already hurt from the loud booms, but she couldn't slow down.

Webster's life depended on it.

"I've got to get this rope untied," she rushed.

Finally, she had an idea. She grabbed the headband from her head and broke off the weapon-like "building" she'd been complaining about all day. She began to use it to saw against the rope.

It was working.

But she glanced at her watch. Half the show was over.

If she wasn't careful, she wouldn't finish in time.

She had heard about accidents at firework displays before. What if some of the sparks from the other fireworks somehow caught these on fire before it was time?

Otherwise, she could try to stop whoever was supposed to light this.

But if it was Chad Morrison, there was no hope.

She worked harder.

As she did, she glanced back.

Scoops still sat there, staring at her. She was so grateful the canine was loyal, but right now she needed for him to go away.

"Get Cassidy," she told Scoops.

The dog's ears rose.

"That's right, boy. Get Cassidy." She had no idea if the dog understood what she was saying.

The next moment, Scoops took off across the sand.

Relief stretched across her chest. Maybe her dog would be okay, at least.

The rope was slowly fraying. She just needed to work it a bit more.

"Serena . . ." Webster muttered.

"It's going to be okay," she told him. "I'm going to get you out of this."

"But if you don't . . ."

"Don't talk like that," she said. "This is going to work."

The rack right beside them sent flashes of light streaming into the air. With each boom, Serena flinched. Her muscles tightened even more.

Finally, her makeshift knife broke through the rope.

It had worked!

She grabbed Webster's hand. "Come on."

They both ran down the beach, away from the fireworks. Just as the rack Webster had been tied to erupted, they fell into the sand.

They were safe.

But as the thought entered her head, she sensed someone's presence near her.

She looked up to see Chad Morrison standing there.

CHAPTER TWENTY-ONE

"YOU WEREN'T SUPPOSED to be here," he growled.

Serena scooted away from him, doing a crab crawl through the sand as she tried to put space between them.

"How could you do this?" Serena asked.

"He got my sister fired." Chad glared at Webster.

Serena glanced at Webster, waiting for an explanation.

"It's true," Webster said. "His half-sister worked for Sky Gourmet. She was one of the people who lost their jobs because of my article."

"And she hasn't been the same since then. In fact, she hasn't been able to hold down a job. She was just starting to get back on her feet after a bad relationship. I really don't like it when people mess with my little sister."

"You were the one who set those bombs up in Richmond also?" Serena asked.

"I couldn't let those people at Sky Gourmet get away with what they did. It was wrong. And our lawsuit was thrown out. Someone needed to pay."

"So why did you decide to turn all your vengeance on Webster?" Serena asked.

At least she was buying time.

In theory.

"If he hadn't done that article, she would still have a job right now."

"But it would be a job where she worked terrible hours for little pay and in bad conditions," Serena said. "Is that really what you wanted?"

His nostrils flared. "He should have minded his own business."

"I was only trying to help," Webster said. "I never meant for any of that to happen."

"Now I'm going to ruin you," Chad said. "Since my little fireworks accident didn't pan out, I'm going to have to think of something else."

"Isn't it already bad enough that you set me up to take the fall for all your pipe bombs?" Webster asked.

"I'm afraid the police might see through that. There could be a way I could make you look guilty and like you couldn't handle it anymore. Like you took your own life. I still have some fireworks left. I can make it look like you got nosy and then had a serious accident."

"You don't want to do that," Serena said.

"And why not?" Chad asked.

"Right now, you're just guilty of sending threats," Serena said. "But if anyone dies . . . you'll be a murderer. How are you going to help your sister from prison?"

His gaze darkened. "I'll figure out something."

"But will you?" Serena continued. "How are you going to do that if you don't have any income? You can't support her that way."

"Shut up!" Chad's anger was obviously rising. "I don't want to talk about this anymore. Now I need the two of you to get up. I need to come up with a Plan B."

"Aren't your guys going to be looking for you?" Serena asked.

"I own this company. I oversee the operations. Right now, my guys are cleaning up, something they're very capable of doing without me."

So much for that idea . . . Serena's mind raced to try to come up with another plan.

But when she saw Chad's gun shining in the moonlight, she knew she was in trouble.

"I said stand up," Chad growled.

Webster and Serena both pulled themselves to their feet. Sand clung to their skin, but that didn't matter right now. All that mattered was staying alive.

What were they going to do?

"Move," Chad growled. "Let's find those fireworks left in the truck. There's about to be a tragic accident."

Serena and Webster glanced at each other.

Her original plan had bombed. Now she could only hope that Chad's would too.

A FEW MINUTES LATER, Serena and Webster were trudging across the sand. Chad walked behind them, gun in hand and a promise that if they slipped up, they would get a bullet before they got the explosion.

"I'm thinking this is how the story will go," Chad muttered. "The two of you got nosy and started to snoop around my truck. That's when there was a tragic accident. Some of the fireworks I left in the back went off. The damage to your bodies after the explosion would be so bad that I doubt the coroner would be able to find any bullet damage."

"Then you don't know Clemson," Webster said. "He's a great medical examiner."

"Whatever you say," Chad muttered. "Now walk."

They continued toward the truck in the distance.

As they did, Serena glanced around. There was absolutely nobody else around here. Thanks to this area being closed off to any spectators, there was also no one around to help.

What was she going to do? She kept asking herself that question. And she would continue to ask herself that question until she thought of an idea to save them.

She spotted the truck. It had Chad's company's name written on the side of it.

And, sure enough, none of his crew was here yet. No doubt they were all on the beach still trying to clean up the remnants of the firework display.

A firetruck was also parked in the distance, with the fire marshal here to oversee everything. But they were far enough away that none of the firefighters would see them.

Panic surged through her.

This wasn't looking good.

"The two of you, sit on the back of the truck. One move, and I'll pull the trigger," Chad said.

Serena and Webster glanced at each other one more time. Then they did as he said.

But Serena would almost rather die of a gunshot wound than of a fireworks explosion. At least that way, people would know that something had happened. That it hadn't been an accident.

Was that how Webster felt? She didn't want to get him killed in this process.

They sat on the edge of the truck. As they did, Chad began to play with something in the back of it. And then he pulled out a blowtorch.

Serena knew they didn't have much time.

"Webster, run!" she yelled.

It was almost like he had been on the same wavelength she was. They both took off across the parking lot, willing to take their chances.

"Stop right there before I shoot!"

Serena braced herself for the feel of the bullet piercing her flesh.

But before she felt any pain, she heard a new voice.

"Put your hands in the air," a female said. "Police!"

She turned her head and saw Cassidy and two of her officers standing there, guns pointed at Chad.

And coming from behind Cassidy was Scoops.

The little dog ran right into Serena's arms and began to lick her face.

"Oh, Scoops. You're okay. Good boy."

Webster reached in and rubbed the dog's back also. "I do believe this dog is your guardian angel."

Serena wasn't going to argue with that.

CHAPTER TWENTY-TWO

AS CHAD WAS LED AWAY in handcuffs, Serena looked up at Webster.

"I'm glad you're okay," she muttered.

"Me too. Thank you."

"I owed you one."

A small smile tugged at his lips. "I guess we're even then."

She shifted, Scoops still in her arms. If she had her way, she might never let the dog go.

"So what happened tonight?" she asked.

"I was just standing there on the boardwalk waiting for you when Chad approached me. He had a gun beneath his jacket and told me to come with him or I'd regret it."

Serena frowned. "I'm sorry."

"No, *I'm* sorry."

"Do you regret writing that article?"

"I regret the consequences. But I still think exposing greedy men's evil actions was the right thing. Sometimes the right actions can still have the wrong consequences, though."

His words made a lot of sense. Serena had lived that out on more than one occasion.

Cassidy walked up to them. "Are you two doing okay? Are you sure I can't take you to the clinic?"

"We're fine," Serena said. "It's just a good thing you showed up when you did."

"I got your message from Paige, but I didn't know exactly where to find you. Thankfully, I saw Scoops, and he led me right to you."

Serena hugged the dog close again. "He is the best dog ever."

"I can't argue with that," Cassidy said. "But don't tell Kujo."

Kujo was Cassidy's dog.

"So what's going to happen to Chad now?" Serena asked.

"He's going to be going away to jail for a long time. I'm going to need to get statements from both of you. But I'm glad that you're both okay."

"So are we," Webster said. "Does this mean I've been cleared of any charges?"

"Maybe not officially on paper yet, but I have a feeling this is all going to be behind you very soon."

"That's something to be happy about, at least."

"I'd say so too," Serena said. "So what now? Do we need to go down to the station?"

"That would be great," Cassidy said.

"How about if I bring us all some Popsicles to brighten the mood?"

"Popsicles?" Cassidy asked.

"I'm thinking some Bomb Pops might be good."

Webster and Cassidy groaned.

As they did, Serena fought a smile.

They'd just closed another case.

What wasn't there to be happy about?

COMING NEXT: BANANA SPLIT PERSONALITIES

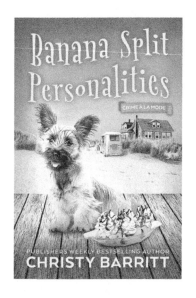

ALSO BY CHRISTY BARRITT:

THE WORST DETECTIVE EVER:

I'm not really a private detective. I just play one on TV.

Joey Darling, better known to the world as Raven Remington, detective extraordinaire, is trying to separate herself from her invincible alter ego. She played the spunky character for five years on the hit TV show *Relentless*, which catapulted her to fame and into the role of Hollywood's sweetheart. When her marriage falls apart, her finances dwindle to nothing, and her father disappears, Joey finds herself on the Outer Banks of North Carolina, trying to piece together her life away from the limelight. But as people continually mistake her for the character she played on TV, she's tasked with solving real life crimes . . . even though she's terrible at it.

ABOUT THE AUTHOR

USA Today has called Christy Barritt's books "scary, funny, passionate, and quirky."

Christy writes both mystery and romantic suspense novels that are clean with underlying messages of faith. Her books have won the Daphne du Maurier Award for Excellence in Suspense and Mystery, have been twice nominated for the Romantic Times Reviewers' Choice Award, and have finaled for both a Carol Award and Foreword Magazine's Book of the Year.

She is married to her Prince Charming, a man who thinks she's hilarious—but only when she's not trying to be. Christy is a self-proclaimed klutz, an avid music lover who's known for spontaneously bursting into song, and a road trip aficionado.

When she's not working or spending time with her family, she enjoys singing, playing the guitar, and exploring small, unsuspecting towns where people have no idea how accident-prone she is.

Find Christy online at:
www.christybarritt.com
www.facebook.com/christybarritt
www.twitter.com/cbarritt

Sign up for Christy's newsletter to get information on all of her latest releases here: **www. christybarritt.com/newsletter-sign-up/**

If you enjoyed this book, please consider leaving a review.

COMPLETE BOOK LIST

Squeaky Clean Mysteries:

#13 Cold Case: Clean Getaway

#14 Cold Case: Clean Sweep

#15 Cold Case: Clean Break

#16 Cleans to an End (coming soon)

While You Were Sweeping, A Riley Thomas Spinoff

The Sierra Files:

#1 Pounced

#2 Hunted

#3 Pranced

#4 Rattled

The Gabby St. Claire Diaries (a Tween Mystery series):

The Curtain Call Caper

The Disappearing Dog Dilemma

The Bungled Bike Burglaries

The Worst Detective Ever

#1 Ready to Fumble

#2 Reign of Error

#3 Safety in Blunders

#4 Join the Flub

#5 Blooper Freak

#6 Flaw Abiding Citizen

#7 Gaffe Out Loud

#8 Joke and Dagger

#9 Wreck the Halls

#10 Glitch and Famous (coming soon)

Raven Remington

Relentless 1

Relentless 2 (coming soon)

Holly Anna Paladin Mysteries:

#1 Random Acts of Murder

#2 Random Acts of Deceit

#2.5 Random Acts of Scrooge

#3 Random Acts of Malice

#4 Random Acts of Greed

#5 Random Acts of Fraud

#6 Random Acts of Outrage

#7 Random Acts of Iniquity

Lantern Beach Mysteries

#1 Hidden Currents

#2 Flood Watch

#3 Storm Surge

#4 Dangerous Waters

#5 Perilous Riptide

#6 Deadly Undertow

Lantern Beach Romantic Suspense

Tides of Deception

Shadow of Intrigue

Storm of Doubt

Winds of Danger

Rains of Remorse

Lantern Beach P.D.

On the Lookout

Attempt to Locate

First Degree Murder

Dead on Arrival

Plan of Action

Lantern Beach Escape

Afterglow (a novelette)

Lantern Beach Blackout

Dark Water

Safe Harbor

Ripple Effect

Rising Tide

Crime á la Mode

Deadman's Float

Milkshake Up

Bomb Pop Threat (coming soon)

Banana Split Personalities (coming soon)

The Sidekick's Survival Guide

The Art of Eavesdropping

The Perks of Meddling

The Exercise of Interfering

The Practice of Prying (coming soon)

Carolina Moon Series

Home Before Dark

Gone By Dark

Wait Until Dark

Light the Dark

Taken By Dark

Suburban Sleuth Mysteries:

Death of the Couch Potato's Wife

Fog Lake Suspense:

Edge of Peril

Margin of Error

Brink of Danger

Line of Duty

Cape Thomas Series:

Dubiosity

Disillusioned

Distorted

Standalone Romantic Mystery:

The Good Girl

Suspense:

Imperfect

The Wrecking

Sweet Christmas Novella:

Home to Chestnut Grove

Standalone Romantic-Suspense:

Keeping Guard

The Last Target

Race Against Time

Ricochet

Key Witness

Lifeline

High-Stakes Holiday Reunion

Desperate Measures

Hidden Agenda

Mountain Hideaway

Dark Harbor

Shadow of Suspicion

The Baby Assignment

The Cradle Conspiracy

Trained to Defend

Nonfiction:

Characters in the Kitchen

Changed: True Stories of Finding God through Christian Music (out of print)

The Novel in Me: The Beginner's Guide to Writing and Publishing a Novel (out of print)

Made in United States
Orlando, FL
06 February 2024

43353471R00114